The Fargoer

The Farqoer

Book I of the Farqoer Chronicles

Petteri Hannila

Translated from the Finnish novel "Kaukamoinen".
Copyright (C) 2013 Petteri Hannila
Layout design and Copyright (C) 2019 by Next Chapter
Published 2019 by Shadow City – A Next Chapter Imprint
Cover art by Cover Mint
Translation: Peitsa Suoniemi, Miika Hannila, Petteri Hannila
Editor (Finnish): Jenny Peräaho (Kirjalabyrintti)
Editors (English): Peitsa Suoniemi, Anthony Farnden, Lorna Read
Additional editors: Joanne Asala, Ben Gold, Danielle Smith-Scott

Contents

*Dedicated to those
who know that giving up
is not an option.*

End of Innocence

Walkers in the Forest

UMMER SUN scorched the wilderness beyond the unknown expanse. Two girls moved through the forest with sure steps, although no trails or signs of men were visible to guide their way. The girls looked so much alike that they could have been sisters. Both were slim and short, as women of the Kainu tended to be. Their long hair was as dark as the autumn evening and stood out from their pale, clear skin. Only their noses and cheekbones were slightly tanned by the scorch of the summer.

The girls were sweating despite only wearing light shoes and belts made of deerskin. From their belts dangled roughly-chiseled stone knives sheathed in leather. The Kainu knew iron, but its use was inappropriate for the task at hand. So they'd been given the stone knives for this age-old tradition, a tradition that dated back a long way, to the gloom of history. Countless girls before them had carried those same knives on the same path that led them now. The girls had both seen thirteen summers. As they had each started to bleed, they were now ready to draw blood and reach maturity.

Despite their many similarities, the girl running ahead was more heavily built, and her brown eyes shone with a sense of nobility befitting a chieftain's daughter. Even at such a young age, Aure was used to giving commands and getting what she wanted. Not too far behind her ran Vierra, and what she lacked in nobility and stature, she made up for with tenacity and sheer stubbornness. In her deep-green eyes glimmered a determination and optimism typical of the young. The girls had played together since they were babies, and had remained best friends throughout their childhood.

Normally, a trip to the woods like this would have been filled with the girls' endless chatter and the occasional laugh. Now, however, they were silent, and filled with anticipation and excitement. They had waited for this day as the deer wait for the spring. Finally, they would take the crucial step that would carry them from their childhood play into the world of adults.

The hot afternoon sun forced them to slow their pace. Summer had been exceptionally warm, and the region was as dry as dust. Gray rocks, yellow shrubs, and tussocks, some still green, were mixed among murky tree roots. Rays of light beamed through the branches, scattering the colors into a flickering and tattered shambles. The buzz of the horseflies and the singing of the birds made music for the spectacle. The forest floor was pocketed with islets of musty air and the strong, suffocating stench of plants. Nature was slowly withering, waiting for rain.

The girls' eyes were looking for signs of water in the dry woods. Finally, they found a river that had dried out to a meager stream. It slowly snaked in between the large rocks and drew the girls irresistibly. The trickling sound and the soft breeze tempted them to rest. The plants near the stream were lush and verdant, and Vierra and Aure had to clear their way through the bushes to reach the water.

Between the rocks, in the knee-deep waters of the creek, was one of the few places that the relentless heat couldn't reach. The girls drank greedily and drenched themselves in the cool water. Normally, a hot day like this would have been spent swimming, fishing, and maybe even bickering over who had the larger catch. Now, there was no time for swimming, nor would it have been possible in the shallow stream. But something else in the forest was also thirsty. While the girls were drinking, a bear cub emerged from the thicket. It came from upwind and didn't notice the bathing girls until it was only twenty paces away. It froze, too afraid to run away or come closer, and let loose a miserable call.

The girls felt the cold whisper of death shiver up their spines as they saw the cub. Where there was a cub, the mother was never too far away. They crept to the opposite shore, keeping their eyes on the animal and the thicket from which it had emerged. It was hard to walk backwards in the rocky stream. Painfully, slowly, and carefully, they ascended from the bottom to the bank, until they reached the border of the nearby thicket.

The bushes started to rustle, and all of a sudden the mother bear came rushing up, head down, through the shrub to its offspring. It ran to the creek and, upon seeing the girls, rose on its hind legs and released a roar that froze the girls' blood in their veins. Unfortunately, their escape options were few; darting headlong into the woods would have been hopeless, for no one can outrun an angry mother bear. On the other hand, staying put was equally dangerous, since a stone knife in the hands of a young girl wouldn't stop the beast.

Luckily, the bear didn't attack; at least not immediately. It towered above the girls on its hind legs in the stream and snapped its jaws menacingly. The girls were trapped, too afraid to move, stuck in a heart-pounding stalemate. The bear was puzzled; these people were small and didn't stink of fire and death. They had no spears, either, which the bear knew to be a threat.

"We can't stand here forever. I'm going to retreat to the thicket," said Vierra finally.

"Don't go... let's sing a soothing song," replied Aure. The confidence that normally filled her voice was gone, replaced by panic and fear.

"Alright, let's try."

They started. At first, the sound was pitifully weak, and the girls felt that their fear and the riverside rocks swallowed it whole. But the bear stopped its attack and slowly, the girls grew brave enough to sing louder. Harder and harder they sang until the sound was echoing among the rocks, feeding their courage.

> *Ruler of the darkest forest*
> *Wanderer of the hidden path*
> *Sister of the humankind*
> *Spare us from your deadly wrath*
>
> *Do not grab with paws so mighty*
> *Fasten not your jaws*
> *Show us not your immense power*
> *Rest your fangs and claws*
>
> *Let the fellow-dweller pass by*
> *Release us from this bind*

Whether it was the power of the song or something more mundane, the girls couldn't tell. Nevertheless, the bear dropped down on all fours and herded its young back into the thicket. Soon after the mother disappeared, silence fell over the forest once more as though nothing had ever happened. It took much longer for the girls' hearts to calm down.

"There's something to tell over the home fire," said Vierra, with a look of relief on her face.

"You will tell no one," Aure snapped. "We're not allowed to tell anything of the journey, not a word. Don't you remember?"

"I know," Vierra sighed.

When their legs could carry them again, they continued their journey through the sweltering forest.

The Mother

Afternoon was giving way to evening as the girls arrived at a swampy lakeshore. The summer had dried up the beach, leaving only a carpet of moss that grew all the way to the waterfront. Despite the boggy southern edge, the lake had clear water from the many springs that fed it from the bottom. Nobody fished the lake because it was a holy place. Only girls who had reached womanhood came here, and then only once in their lives, during the hottest period of the summer. After their visit, they returned to their people as women and took their place among the adults. Before this, they had to face the First Mother, who weighed every girl's right to adulthood. Aure and Vierra were here for this very reason, and upon their return, they would be celebrated around the fires of their people.

It sometimes happened that a girl sent to become a woman never returned from her voyage.

Vierra and Aure cut straight, slim branches from the bushes surrounding the swamp and sharpened them into spears with their stone knives. They were crude weapons, but for their purpose they were perfect. After finishing the spears, the girls went to the water's edge, a bit away from each other, and stepped into the shallows. Sunlight had warmed the surface, but on the bottom, the lake was cooler and brought relief to the girls' weary feet. After wading a little deeper, they stopped and stood in the still, shallow water with their spears. The horseflies, fat from the heat of summer, thoroughly enjoyed this game, and soon both girls had several bite marks on their bodies. Gritting their teeth, they stood still and let the pests go about their business.

Soon, small fish began circling around them, curious and unafraid of the large, stationary figures. When nothing happened, few bigger fish followed the small ones, entering the girls' reach.

Aure was the luckier of the two, spearing a big, thick-necked perch. Vierra wasn't far behind: her catch was a small adolescent pike that had wandered within the spear's range. The girls took their stone knives and gutted the fish with care. To slake their thirst, they drank from the lake. The water had a stale taste burned into it by the sun during the hot summer days. Relieved nonetheless, they stood on the beach and waited, shooing away the horseflies. Now, they wouldn't have to greet the Mother without an offering.

The scorching sun was setting toward the horizon. The evening cooled the air down to a bearable warmth, and the horseflies disappeared only to be replaced by mosquitoes, forcing the girls to slap and flail continuously to drive them away. They missed the protection of their leather clothes, but clothes were forbidden, as initiates couldn't have in their possession anything that had been taken from another living creature when in the presence of the First Mother. Besides their belts and shoes only a stone knife and an offering were allowed. After the sun had set, dusk quickly took over. This far north, the midsummer sun wouldn't have allowed the darkness to set in, even in the middle of the night, but, this late in the summer, it would soon give way to the black of night.

"I wonder if it's true what they say about the boat," said Aure, breaking the long silence.

"I hope it comes soon. Otherwise it'll be so dark that we won't see it, no matter how strange it is."

"If the old hags say that the boat will come, then it'll come."

"I guess so." Vierra laughed uneasily. "It will have to have torches burning on it, anyway, if it doesn't arrive soon."

Long before dark, the shadowy shape of a boat appeared on the tranquil, open lake. The girls went to the shore and waited nervously. As the boat approached, they saw that it was of plain and simple design, its wooden surface worn smooth by age. There were no oars or oarsmen, but everywhere around it water rose up in frothy waves. With a splash, the boat glided onto the shore and surged onto the mossy bank.

"On board, then," Aure stated and stepped to the back of the boat without hesitation. The glance she threw back to Vierra didn't display the confidence of her words, however. Vierra followed, not saying anything. Each sought comfort from the other's eyes, their gazes flitting back and forth. If they had been competitive earlier, they were in this together now.

The mysterious old boat slowly slid away from the beach and back into the open lake. The girls heard splashing behind the stern, but neither one dared to look for the source. Unlike other ancient vessels, this old boat had no trace of leaks or cracks and traveled steadily forward, smelling of tangy resin and soil.

A pair of swans was making a stir on the lake, splashing their strong wings against the water and driving a younger intruder away from their nesting place. A loon with its offspring floated with poise on the dark water and started to feed. The night birds were singing, and the lake was full of life as the boat took the girls towards a small, craggy island. The strand was rocky, but the boat glided seamlessly between the rocks and into a grassy cove.

The girls rose from the boat in a hurry and jumped on to the beach. Mosquitoes welcomed them as they entered the withered forest. The strip of spruce was narrow, and the rocky terrain in the middle of the island was more open. As the girls moved to the north, they neared a steep cliff. When they reached its base, an ominous stone wall loomed in front of them. They had no gear, and the burdens of the day weighed in their limbs.

"Who's first to the top of the cliff?" yelled Aure in challenge, and she stormed to the ridge without waiting for an answer. Vierra yelled and dashed after her friend with whatever strength her tired legs had in them. For a moment, they were just two girls competing again.

Sweating and gasping, the girls pulled themselves to the top. The hasty climb without the protection of clothes had left bruises and marks on their hands and feet.

"I won!" Aure yelled, with a familiar mischievousness on her face. She nudged Vierra playfully on the shoulder as she climbed beside her to the mountaintop. Vierra, exhausted, couldn't say a word, but her green eyes flashed her opinion on losing.

"You cheated, you took a head start," Vierra snorted, once her breath had evened out. Aure had already turned her focus elsewhere.

I will best you yet, Vierra thought, but didn't say it out loud.

The summit was flat, and a beautiful view opened up to the slowly darkening lake. The path that led the girls up the cliff top was uneven, but all of the other edges were straight and steep, with a fall of at least a full-grown tree's worth onto the beach below. The middle of the plateau was covered with the soot of previous fires, and a stone axe sat beside a pile of firewood, though no tinder could be seen.

"Nothing to start the fire with," said Vierra, in a tired voice. She realized how arduous it would be to get a fire going.

"Like the old ones say, wood against wood."

"And with words of fire," Vierra added.

The girls went to work. Each started her own fire on top of the cliff, as dictated by tradition, for every girl who was entering adulthood had to have her own fire. They chose two of the driest pieces of wood and cut small notches into them. They whittled additional wood into chaff, and gathered dry moss and grass. This was easy because there was plenty of wood and kindling around, since the rain hadn't touched the area for many weeks. They placed a piece of wood on top of the campfire rock and started to saw on it sideways, using another notched piece of wood. Their furious sawing heated up the wood and a thin, black wisp of smoke rose from the spot they were sawing. The girls blew into it and fed it with the dry grass and moss. They also sang the words of *Fire's Birth* to lure its spirit to them.

> *Oh, you Seagull, bird of birds*
> *Strengthen here our pyre*
> *Termes mighty, lord of heavens*
> *Bring to us your fire*
>
> *Give me now the brand of yellow*
> *Spark of highest heat*
> *Warmth to lonely forest dweller*
> *Flame of life unsheathe*

Both girls' patches of moss lit almost at the same time, burning with a small, withering wisp. They fed the fire eagerly with wood shavings until the pile burst into flames. The fire crackled and smoked from the resin within the wood. Dirty and sweaty from the work, the girls were happy nonetheless, as the smoke drove away the mosquitoes and the fire dispelled the feeling of uneasiness that came with the dark. They placed the fish on the tips of their spears and cooked them in the fire. The air was filled with anticipation as the late summer night fell upon them.

"My fish is bigger than yours," Vierra blurted from behind her campfire. She hadn't forgotten the sting of defeat from the climb.

"Pike tastes like mud compared to perch," Aure replied. "Mother will take my present first."

"Surely she will not. You always burn your fish black. Nobody can eat them."

It was hard to say from where she arrived to the fire. Neither Aure nor Vierra saw her approach. Like the girls, she wore only a leather belt, and her sparse hair was tied back with a string. But that was the end of the resemblance. Her extreme old age was evident, as her parched skin was dark and filled with wrinkles. Countless infants had nursed her breasts flat and left them hanging down her skinny sides. As dark as her limbs were, her face was even darker and protruded with a crooked jaw that had only a few teeth left. Despite her wretched appearance, her gaze was sharp as a blade, and a sense of power and wisdom surrounded her. She smelled strongly of resin and the forest, just like the boat that had carried the girls to the island.

At first she said nothing, and shoved her worn hands towards the girls. They looked at each other and then gave their cooked fish to the hag, watching silently as she ate them in the glow of the fire. She made no distinction between pike or perch, but ate the catch complete with tails, heads, and bones, swallowing them in big chunks. After this meal, she rubbed her hands together, obviously pleased, and spoke.

"Aure, Vierra," she started, her voice as deep as it was solemn. "As girls you came here, and as women you wish to leave. But first you must hear of the birth of your people, and then we will see your worth." She started to sing, her worn voice filled with an energy and raw power that belied her age and appearance.

The song began calmly, telling of the birth of the world. The Mother sang a story of a seagull that looked for a nesting place on the shoreless sea, and finally found a rock that pushed through the surface. The song strengthened as it portrayed the rising rage of the sea and the wave that destroyed the seagull's nest, throwing the eggs into the merciless ocean. It gained a sense of wonder as the seagull sang a crafting song, a song of great magic. From the pieces of the eggs, the wise bird made the world and the sky to cover it. The song gave birth to all plants, animals, and men. For every creature, the seagull made a mate, save for humankind, for they were seeds of sorrow and the source of all evil. Finally, the sea took up the task and created a woman for the man. But this woman, the First Woman, would not bow at the man's feet, but became instead the ruler of the land, the guardian of her people.

The girls listened to the song, mesmerized. They had heard it before, but the Mother's voice was different and it carried them through these stormy events. It made the girls forget their excitement and fear for a moment, and they let the tale take them somewhere else, to another place and time in the distant past. Finally, the song died down, allowing the girls to wake up and return to reality.

After singing, the old woman stood up from beside the fire and continued.

"Remember this song and sing it to your children by a fire, like your mothers have surely sung to you. Now we shall see what kind of women you really are."

She approached them, first Aure and then Vierra, and examined them roughly from head to toe, grunting occasionally with approval.

"You will both make good mothers, but only one can be the chieftain. Aure, you are the chieftain's daughter. Vierra is the chieftain's niece, and not unworthy to the task. However, the ruler is not chosen by her bloodline but rather by her actions. Here, you are equal."

Her gaze gained cold determination as she continued.

"If you, Aure, become the leader, our kind will prosper at first, but people in surrounding areas will eventually come, and the Kainu shall disappear forever. If you, Vierra, are chosen, our people will suffer greatly but shall be preserved for as long as my eyes can see. In this, I have a serious decision, because if Aure comes back from here alive, she will become the leader. Those of us who have survived have always been tough and resilient, and I say now to fight until only one of you is left. The survivor will be the chieftain after Aure's mother passes."

This cruel suggestion was left hanging in the air, and the girls stared at each other, trying to read each other's intentions. Aure jumped up, drew the stone blade from her belt and approached Vierra with a grim look on her face. She wouldn't let anything come between her and her prize. Vierra got up nimbly and backed away from her cousin's knife. Their eyes met briefly over the gloom of the campfires. In their stare was something new, something that hadn't been there even in their worst quarrels. Something that could not be found in the eyes of a child.

They started a round of a dangerous game in the blaze of the fires. There was very little space to move around in: falling from the edge would mean a plunge downwards in the dark to the waiting rocks below. Vierra backed away for a while but finally had to let her cousin come close for fear of falling down. They grabbed each other, weapons in hand, and were soon rolling on the rocky cliff top, wrestling for their lives. They tumbled over Vierra's fire, spewing flames and a high spout of sparks as the burning wood moved violently. Both had wrestled almost as long as they had breathed, and they were equally matched in skill. Still, Aure's sturdiness gave her an edge, and she managed to push her cousin's knife hand to the ground as they struggled on the edge of the cliff. Aure's knife slowly approached Vierra's throat, inch by inch, until the jagged edge almost touched the glistening, sweaty skin. Shaking, they were both frozen in this position for a brief moment, and neither one seemed to be able to move forward.

Vierra swooped Aure off from on top of her in one swift motion, causing Aure to fall headfirst over the cliff's edge. Before Aure plunged down to her death, Vierra grabbed her by the arm. Aure's stone knife slipped from her grasp and clattered onto the rocks below, as she dangled in midair, held by her cousin. The girls gazed at each other, their eyes flashing with lightning in the dark. From the background came the eerie voice of the Mother.

"Let her go, Vierra. You will be the chieftain, and our people will live forever."

For a brief moment, Vierra could not reach a decision. She looked into her cousin's eyes and remembered their friendship, the runs they had made through the forests while the village men nodded their approval, saying to one another, "Such great women they will be, but which one will lead?" She remembered how their differences and disputes had grown when they got older. Aure had tried to bend Vierra to her will, as she had bent all the other children of the tribe. Like a small chieftain, she had given orders in their games and chores as the adults watched from the side, amused. But Vierra hadn't approved of her rule and hadn't given in an inch. And when the spirits had taken Vierra's parents to them, one after another, and Aure's mother had taken the orphaned girl under her wing, the competition between them had risen to a completely new level. Besides the authority, they now also had a common mother from whom they both wanted admiration and attention.

Nobody would blame Vierra if she allowed Aure to fall to her death. The Mother was positively demanding it of her. She would get everything that Aure now had. She would be chieftain, and the Kainu would be preserved forever. Aure would definitely not save her, if it was the other way around.

Vierra yanked Aure back up to the surface with both hands and shouted, "This is enough! I won't kill my cousin, no matter who tells me to do so, not even if it is you, Mother. In the morning I will leave, with or without your blessing."

The night air was cut with a rising, low-pitched laugh from the Mother's throat.

"The chieftain's blood truly runs in your veins. You both will have my blessing, of course. You have brought honor both to yourselves and to your people. Never again shall you enter the children's hut."

The Mother fell silent, and neither of the girls said anything, either. Aure drew a heavy breath and avoided Vierra's gaze, a rare, secluded look on her face. They revived their fires as the burdens of the day started to slowly take their toll. Both tried to stay awake, but finally sleep took over. The last thing Vierra saw with her sleepy eyes was the Mother, poking the fire with a gentle smile on her wrinkly face.

The First and the Last

Vierra winced awake and noticed she was lying in the entrance of an opening that led inside the cliff. Underneath her, she could feel the cold surface of the rock, and behind her twinkled the bare, star-filled sky. Further in, somewhere in the depths of the corridor, she could see a fluttery gleam of light. Vierra got up and approached it cautiously. Soon, the corridor opened up into a big cave. In the middle was a fire, and behind the flames was the Mother. She stood facing the wall, away from Vierra, painting the wall with a color as red as blood. The huge walls of the cave were covered in pictures of men, animals, and life. There were the deer, the salmon, and the moose, the most important game for the Kainu. Amid them were the gallant wolf, bear, and wolverine. The entire history of the tribe was painted on the walls. In one place they hunted, in another they loved, and here and there the children ran around playfully. The gloom of the fire made the wall paintings flicker and overlap. Some showed battles against men or beasts, in which the red paint looked very like blood. The changing light made one picture disappear, only to reveal another one beneath it. In turn, this one also disappeared and made way for a third. The movements of the lively flames made Vierra doubt her eyes, and she blinked furiously to clear them.

Listening carefully, Vierra could make out voices. The pictures were alive! People were talking and animals grunting. Here and there, children laughed or cried. As Vierra kept looking, the voices became louder and more numerous until they completely filled her head and she had to close her eyes.

The Mother turned towards Vierra, and her wrinkled face was full of surprise.

"What are you doing here? It is not your time yet."

"I don't know. I must be dreaming."

"This is no dream. There must be a reason that you are here, though. You must know because you are the last."

"The last what?"

"The last of the Kainu, the last Mother. The greatest of us all, and yet still so small and powerless. Everybody else I will paint onto this wall, but in time, you will paint yourself. Then our story will have been told in its entirety, and we will all meet by the fires of the Underworld. You will paint it there," said the Mother, pointing at the only empty spot on the cave walls. It was entirely surrounded by pictures of women. There were noble young women armed with spears and bows. There were wrinkly old women sitting by their campfires. Others were giving birth, bringing new life to this world. Some dried fish in the strong winds in between winter and spring.

"What do I have to do?" asked Vierra. The fate of their tribe was making her uneasy. She could feel how tiny and insignificant she was in the middle of these majestic walls that surrounded her. "Why isn't Aure here? Isn't it she who will be the chieftain?"

"I do not know," said the Mother, laughing in a tone that was not at all encouraging. "And even if I did, it is not my place to say. Your cousin's path is not yours to travel."

"And why did you take my father and mother? Why didn't you take anything from Aure?"

"The Fargoer does not have a mother, the Wanderer does not have a father. When you have to decide, decide well. When you can't affect things, bear them. When you do well, do not stop and rejoice because the next challenge will come soon and pass you by. You will perform great deeds, but your path will also be filled with great pain and sorrow. Songs of such deeds are not sung around Kainu campfires, but it doesn't make them meaningless."

"That means nothing," Vierra replied. She tried to keep her anger at bay out of respect to the walls, rather than the Mother.

"That is true. Luckily, your life's troubles are not my troubles. Sleep now, but remember everything, especially this cave. You will know when it is time." And Vierra's eyes closed, and no dream reached her again that night.

The girls awoke to the buzzing of flies. The fires had gone out a good while ago and the sun had risen in the cloudless sky, boding another hot day. However, there was a dark front of thunder far on the horizon, like a huge, steep line of mountains. The girls got up and quickly readied themselves for their journey home. Both had wide smiles across their faces. Like any children, they quickly forgot the bad things they had suffered and nurtured the good things in their minds. They would be considered adults now, and would soon be celebrated by the hut fires of their people. Their young minds couldn't yet anticipate what adulthood would bring with it. As they climbed down the cliff towards the strand, their eyes met and their smiles faded. They both knew that the events of the previous evening would be kept a secret.

What had happened on that island had changed them irreversibly, and the joys of childhood had now slipped from their grasp, gone forever.

Autumn Flames

HE DEER-SKIN drum boomed in even rhythm. The sound was held tight by the damp autumn air and didn't reach far outside the camp. Dreary morning rain loosened dying leaves from the trees and spread them out in a carpet, where they waited silently to decay.

The drum boomed the sound of death; the death of a chieftain. A tough woman when in her prime, the chieftain had driven the Turyans and the Vikings from their lands, and kept the southern trappers in order. Still, even she was not immune to the inevitable touch of time. Chronically sick over the summer, she had eventually lapsed to living on the floor of her hut by the time fall arrived.

The tribe's witch, Eera, had been pounding the drum in the dying chieftain's hut since early morning. It would help her journey to the other side and, once started, the witch would not cease until the chieftain was either dead or had regained her health.

Few were allowed in the chieftain's hut during this time. Only the chieftain's daughter, Aure, the witch herself and Eera's apprentice, Rika, were there. The other members of the tribe were not able to carry out their usual deeds and chores. Preparations for the upcoming deer hunt, which took place every fall, would have to wait. The time to move to their winter dwellings drew closer every day. Everything was up in the air now, hanging on the weakening string of life of the suffering chieftain. Whether her condition went one way or the other, it would free the tribe's few dozen men and women to continue their lives. But as long as the drum boomed over the land, nothing would happen.

Vierra didn't listen to the drum. The deathwatch filled her with anguish, so she left the camp and her tribe and went on her way alone. Not even the restless rain delayed her departure, the storm dropping water from the skies like a river. "There goes the Fargoer," the other tribe members whispered. Over the last two summers, the now grown-up Vierra had started to enjoy her solitude. In the winter camps she was silent, and often went to ski and hunt for meat even if it was not needed. In the summertime she disappeared, sometimes for weeks, only to return with as much fish as her slight body could carry. She was the best hunter in the tribe, but the others kept their distance. "She is different, the Fargoer," the hags whispered around the evening fire. And she had taken that name as her own, as if it had been hers to begin with.

On that rainy morning, Vierra didn't go far. She checked the traps she had set the day before. The catch was not good: just a small, skinny fox that was caught in a wooden fox-trap. She finished it off with one well-aimed blow from a club and skinned the animal. It wouldn't taste good, so she gave the skinned carcass to the folk of the earth, setting it on a big anthill. At the same time, she sang:

> *For the men who live below*
> *Under forest, grassy field*
> *Take this gift from uphill servant*
> *Counter evil with your shield*

She finished checking the remaining traps, and the gray day was not yet halfway done. Vierra didn't want to go back to camp, so she did what she had done the day before. Alongside a small forest stream, she had built a rainproof lean-to out of twigs, sprigs, and skins greased with animal fat. There, in her small nest, she kept a fire and did her chores. Now and then, her hand reached to check a line that ended in a wormed hook made of bone – a perfect lure for trout. The stream gave her a couple of fatty treats, which she scorched in the fire on the end of a stick and ate with a ravenous appetite.

Vierra's gaze wandered to the rainy forest, and she felt a familiar sting of longing in her heart. Life was circling around and around on the same trail, the route she knew all too well. The old people said that she should have taken a man by now, maybe two or more, because she was such a good hunter. She had been approached with offers of marriage many times in the winter camps, but she had turned down all of them. Because her mother was dead, according to an old law, nobody could force her to take a man, and so she remained alone. This made her a unique, if frowned-upon, member of the tribe. As such, she had earned another name. Nobody dared to call her "The Frozen Fargoer" openly, but naturally, Vierra found it out. She could not care less. Why raise a family just to fit into the tribe? Everything would eventually be lost, anyway. She often remembered the things told to her by the First Mother, and those things made her no less freezing and no less a Fargoer.

While listening to the rain coming down on her grim thoughts, Vierra heard a sound that broke her out of the gloomy prison of her mind. There was a racket coming from the woods, as if something big was moving through the forest. It could not be any of her tribe; even Rika, who was the worst hunter, did not move so clumsily. Vierra ran through the options in her mind. Maybe a bear or a moose? An autumn-bear would have a lot of fat under its skin, but killing it all by herself would be another matter entirely. Even if she succeeded, the bear spirit would also have to be appeased properly or misfortunes and accidents would be sure to follow. And Eera, who knew the words of appeasing best, was far away in the tribe's camp, hitting the death-drums, and wouldn't leave to sing to spirits while this work was unfinished.

It was no bear, as Vierra soon discovered while peering between the twigs, but a man: a man tall and slender, with hair yellow as swamp-weed burned by summer sun. He looked strange to Vierra, not sturdy like the Vikings although nearly as tall. He staggered towards her, stumbling along the uneven path. When he came closer, Vierra saw the reason: a black-quilled arrow had gone through his thigh, its tip protruding viciously from the front. Finally, a large tree root tripped the staggering man, and he fell headlong into the bushes. Vierra realized that the man was completely spent and could not continue his swaying trek through the forest.

Before she could decide what to do, she heard another sound and realized why the man had tried to run through the bushes although wounded and exhausted. An older man was in pursuit; one who moved with a light step. This one was cast from a different mold to the man he was following: he was short, black-haired, and of good strength. When he spotted the man he was pursuing, he drew from his waistband a sharp-looking blade, as long as an arm. The blade was black and ended in a hook-like, nail-sharp point. Only a few steps separated him from his prey, and all signs were promising the yellow-haired man a quick trip to the fires of the Underworld.

The reason why Vierra then took part in the showdown between these two unknown men completely escaped her. She would ponder that very subject during the following days, but at that moment, she did not hesitate. She pulled an arrow and armed her bow in one smooth, fast movement. In the blink of an eye, she let go the beak of death and it struck the pursuing man in the shoulder. The shaft stuck out grotesquely, and the blade slipped from the man's grip. His face was distorted with pain and amazement, and he fell to his knees on the damp heather.

"One more step, and the next arrow will go through your heart!" yelled Vierra, as if her opponent could have continued the battle. Vierra was astounded, both by the surprising situation and her own, explosive actions. The dark-haired man started a flood of foreign words, which Vierra knew to be Turyan.

The Turyans lived in the north, even though sometimes they wandered in the forests close to the Kainu's heartlands. Every Kainu knew stories of the Turyan people. Most of them painted a picture of feared

Turyan witches and their grudges and blood feuds that lasted for generations. True to their image, this wounded Turyan gathered strength from somewhere. He got up, picked up his blade from the ground and turned away. As he left and slowly vanished into the forest, his voice could still be heard, swearing and cursing in a multitude of languages. The yells echoed in Vierra's ears long after he had disappeared among the trees.

Vierra was snapped out of her thoughts when she realized the light-haired man was trying to get up. She approached him cautiously, her hand ready to grasp a knife or a bow if the situation demanded it. His pale blue eyes were filled with pain and fatigue and it helped put her mind at ease.

"I am Vierra, known as the Fargoer. Hunter and of the chieftain's blood. I walk my mothers' paths as my own. Who are you and why are you pursued by the Turyans? Are you banished, or a slayer of innocents?"

The man managed to crawl up slowly, leaning himself on a small tree. He listened to Vierra's introduction attentively, and then let out a flood of words in a language totally unknown to her. The note and sound of the speech was the same as her own language, but the sentences were strange and didn't make any sense. Here and there, Vierra could pick up a familiar word, but she couldn't attach any meaning to them in her mind. The words "slave," "Turyan," and "Bjarm" were familiar. He continued, and turned to spit a flurry of angry words towards the forest where the black-haired man had retreated. The effort caused the man to stagger and nearly fall over. Vierra quickly offered her arm and supported him to keep him on his feet. Only then did she remember that he was badly injured.

"Come, I have a shelter where we can have a look at your leg."

He did not say anything. Vierra led him through the forest towards the nearby creek where the lean-to was waiting. When they arrived at the shelter, they were both dripping with water and cold. The makeshift building could accommodate only one person, and they had to be very close to each other in order to fit in. The fire had almost died, but Vierra got it to burn again soon enough, despite the rain. The smoking fire wasn't much, but it warmed their limbs nicely and dried the rain.

The man touched his chest and said plainly, "Vaaja."

She nodded. "Now, let me see about that arrow," she replied and ripped the hem from the man's worn pants which were covering the wound. He squeezed his eyes shut and ground his teeth as Vierra examined the injury.

"No bones have been broken, but it has come all the way through. I will cut the arrow and pull the shaft out."

Cutting the shaft was a painful ordeal for Vaaja, as it was sturdy and well-made. Vierra used her knife and sawed the arrow gently from the edge of the point until she could finally break it. Sweat was beading on the man's forehead, even though the weather was rainy and cool.

Pulling the shaft away was too much for the man, and he let out a sharp yell of pain. Blood spewed immediately from the spot where the arrow had come out and Vierra hurried to extinguish the bleeding. Pressing the wound strongly with the hem of his pants, she finally managed to quench the flow.

"Now it doesn't bleed as much. Lie here and stay still, I will be right back." Vierra spoke to the man even though she knew that he had no idea what she was saying. She pressed him down to the covered floor of the lean-to and hoped that he would understand what she meant. Then she disappeared into the rainy forest.

After a moment that felt like an hour, Vierra came back with a multitude of different herbs. She ground them in the rain between two rocks until the plants turned into an even, green paste. She spread the paste carefully into the wound and tightened a wide leather strap over it and around the leg as a bandage.

"There. Nothing more can I do. Now you must rest."

Vaaja spoke in his own tongue, and only then did Vierra notice that he was clothed in rags and very thin, patched clothes. The autumn weather was cool and damp. He wouldn't last long in clothes like that.

"I must get you some decent clothes from our camp. Otherwise, you will freeze and die here, even before the rotting wound would take you."

The man was silent, and took her hand in his own. His grip was strong, and in his pale eyes was a questioning stare, one filled with wariness.

"Do not worry, I will return soon." Vierra squeezed his arm soothingly and looked at him with her deep green eyes. Her reassuring gaze made him smile, and he released his grip.

Fleet as a fox, Vierra traveled through the rainy forest. In her mind were a plethora of questions: Why was he here? Where did he come from? What was she going to do? For a moment, she considered taking him to the tribe's camp to recover. They would be safe there in a warm hut if the black-haired man decided to come back. He couldn't walk when injured this badly, she argued with herself but, deep inside herself, she wondered whether this really was the reason for her decision.

The drum was still pounding in the camp, just as it had been when she left. Her comings and goings were rarely noticed or interfered with. Fellow tribe members were scattered here and there, doing various chores which were largely invented, to fill the time. Vierra gathered some deerskin clothes and dried fish, then stepped hesitantly towards the dying chieftain's hut. For a moment, she just stood in front of it, gathering courage as she considered her options. Finally, she opened the entrance hide.

From the dark interior of the hut, three faces turned to gaze at her: the old and curious witch Eera, the surprised Rika, and the tired and irritated Aure. The chieftain's withered, wax-like face was still. She could no longer raise her head properly from the pillow. The elder's breath ran raspy and intermittent, filling the hut with a distressing, uneven rhythm.

"I am sorry to disturb your peace," Vierra said and bent her head down courteously. "I have wounded my leg and need medicine. Can you help me, Eera?"

"The chieftain's last journey is a sacred act, my child. I do not have time to help you now. Is the wound bad? Show it to me," said Eera. She was an old woman, as old as the chieftain who was slowly withering away on the floor. Eera's long, thin hair was gray, as were her eyes. She was like a skinny and resilient stump that was more tightly attached to life than anyone could imagine.

"I do not want to disturb the ceremony," answered Vierra, trying to hide the insincerity in her voice. "I could get the medicine from your hut, if you tell me where to look. I already treated the wound with grasses and tied it, like you have taught me."

Eera sank back into her thoughts. She had not stopped drumming, not even for a moment. The salmon bone fell on the drum skin again and again, almost as if by itself.

Aure was annoyed, her brown eyes sparked in the dark of the hut. "If the wound is not bad, why do you disturb our peace? Go away!"

Vierra felt a bitter anger boil to the surface. How often had she been driven away in this same fashion? But this time Aure would not get in her way. An angry answer rose to Vierra's lips.

"Soon you will know, too, what it is when the spirits take your mother away."

Vierra had greatly missed her own mother's support, guidance, safety and comfort over the past years. Aure's mother, who was also Vierra's aunt, had taken her into her family, but her real mother was impossible to replace. And a chieftain who was making her own daughter her successor was not the best of foster mothers for a young girl.

Aure took a vehement breath. It had been quite a long time since her last quarrel with Vierra, but now it looked like a storm was brewing again. Tiredness and fear glared from beneath Aure's growing anger. Her mother had been everything to her, as much the subject of her admiration as a reflection of her own future.

Eera intervened. "Do not argue in the hut of death!"

But it wasn't Eera who disrupted their starting argument. The chieftain who lay on the ground suddenly yelled. Truly it was a yell, but it was not a sound that any human could produce. Her feverish, yellow eyes burned like coals for a moment, and the girls instinctively bowed toward her. Her wax-like, skinny and bony hands grabbed both girls' hands and, as if she were summoning her last strength, she guided them shakily together. Soon, the girls noticed that they were holding each other tightly. It was as if all strength escaped from the old woman at that moment, and her limp hands fell to the floor. Only a cackling, abrupt breath told them that the spirit had not yet fully escaped the body.

The girls stood frozen, but Eera did not stay idle.

"Listen carefully, Vierra, and then get out of here and do not come back until the drum stops. Rika will go to my dwelling to fetch you an otter-skin bag. Then you must go to the spring, circle it three times and soothe the sprite, as I have told you. Take water to the pot and boil it by a fire. After that, put a pinch from the bag into the water, and when it has cooled off, drink it. Then your wound will not rot and will be healed fast. Now, be gone!"

The witch's tone did not allow for any argument, and her words broke the moment between Vierra and Aure. Vierra loosened her grip from Aure's hand and left swiftly on her errand, Rika following close behind her.

Rika stepped into the witch's hut and returned almost immediately, carrying an otter-skin bag. She was a plump, red-haired, baby-faced young woman, who wasn't much of a hunter. Her wits were about her, though, so she had become the witch's apprentice. In time, when Eera passed away, she would inherit the witch's role, and with it the powers and responsibilities of the spirit world.

"Aure just seems to keep nagging me, even at her mother's deathbed," Vierra stated briefly, almost as if to herself.

"She's afraid, we're all afraid. What happens when the chieftain dies?" Rika had compassion on her face. This would have irritated Vierra had it come from anyone else but Rika.

"Why do you not limp if there's a bad wound on your leg? I cannot see a bandage, either." Rika changed the subject smoothly.

"I promise I'll tell you later, but now I have no time. It is an important matter, and your herbs will fulfill a great purpose. I did not want to argue and explain in the hut of death."

"Very well," Rika sighed. She was used to Vierra's stubbornness and often gave up easily. There was only one other unmarried woman in the tribe besides her and Vierra and, for this reason, they spent a lot of time together. Vierra never mocked her for her lack of hunting skills, like so many other tribe members did. "I hope I don't get into trouble because of you," Rika added.

"You will not, I promise," Vierra replied and left with the bag.

On the way to the spring, Vierra felt a sting of conscience. She had lied to the witch and to her cousin Aure in the hut where the chieftain was approaching death. Hopefully, the spring sprite would not be angry because of her lie. The man really needed the help of the medicine. She hadn't had time to explain the truth, she reasoned to herself. And the cause was good, and neither the witch nor the chieftain – not even Aure, who was so annoyed – could deny that.

The rain drummed the spring's iron-gray surface. Even the nearby grass had withered, and the seeds in the ground were waiting for new summer. Autumn made all places dreary, even the spring in which the water was considered holy and used only for the most important of purposes. Vierra circled around the spring like the witch had ordered, and sang.

Spring, you beauty, do your duty
Water spirit clear
Give me now your holy water
Power I revere

After she had collected the water, Vierra hurried to her secret lean-to with all her burdens. She was drenched in rainwater and sweat when she arrived, but she wouldn't go to rest. Instead, she offered the thickest leather clothes for Vaaja to wear, and warmed dry fish in the fire for him to eat. He went for the food greedily and silently. When he had eaten, Vierra started to heat up the spring water in the fire with the clay pot she had brought with her. She gestured for the man to lie down when he tried to get up and help. After the water was heated, she mixed the powder into it as Eera had ordered. When the mixture cooled, Vierra offered it to the man. He drank it, grimacing at the taste, and lay down again.

"I will get more wood so it will not run out during the night," said Vierra, before leaving again, like a restless autumn wind.

The day was turning slowly to a dusky evening when Vierra returned to the lean-to, dragging a large, dead tree. The rain that had been going on for days ceased finally, and the cold northern wind started to drive the rain clouds south. The temperature dropped severely as the darkness sneaked over their campsite.

Vierra repaired the lean-to. She delayed her departure until the last glimpse of light, but finally she had to go.

"I will be back in the morning. You will be fine as long as you add wood to the fire occasionally."

"Thank you," said the man, trying to express his gratitude to Vierra in her language. He touched Vierra's black wisps of hair, dirty and wet from the day's chores. A smile found its way to the woman's face. The pain and fear that had been in Vaaja's eyes earlier were gone.

"I will return first thing in the morning."

Vaaja squeezed her hand for goodbye and neither of them said another word. Vierra returned to her tribe's camp and arrived just as the last shimmer of daylight died into a pitch-black night.

The drum in the camp was booming no more, and the chieftain had been carried out of her hut. She lay pale on the bark-decorated bunk. Death had taken both the pain and the energy out of her face, leaving just a fragile old body. In the light of vibrant torches, she could have been easily mistaken for someone who was sleeping peacefully. The tribe members, all the way down to the smallest children, had gathered around their dead leader.

"In the morning, at sunrise, we shall set her on her journey. We need to choose a new chieftain as well, as there are many things to be done before the winter comes." Eera's voice was tired. She would spend most of the coming night negotiating with the spirits. The chieftain deserved the best possible help on her journey to the Underworld.

The honored leader was carried to Eera's hut, which was forbidden to anyone else for the night. Vierra sneaked to the scene like the hunter she was. She didn't want to raise any attention.

"Finally, the Fargoer arrives," said Aure, with scorn in her voice.

"What would I have accomplished here? Would your mother be alive if I had wandered around aimlessly here, like everyone else?"

Aure did not reply, she just turned her back on her cousin. In the flickering torch light, her tear-streaked face looked even dirtier than it was.

The women's hut was nice and warm. The bed skins were dry, and the firewood was gathered into a fine pile near the entrance. In this hut lived the unmarried women, of which there were only two in the tribe besides Vierra. Rika was still helping Eera conduct her ritual matters, but Launi, who took care of the women's hut, had already gone to sleep in her own spot. She was a simple and silent girl, but took care of the hut remarkably well, while Rika spent time studying with Eera and Vierra went about her own solitary business. Such was Launi's spirit that she had never complained to the other girls about the role to which she had been assigned.

Rika finally arrived at the hut and went to her spot, close to Vierra. There was fatigue and evidence of withheld tears in her face. She was an emotional girl, and the day spent with the dying chieftain had not been pleasant. As she lay down to go to sleep, she asked, "Will you tell me now how you used the medicine?"

"It's better that you don't know, so they cannot blame you."

Normally, Rika, who was naturally curious, would have persisted for a long time. But tiredness and being so close to death had debilitated her thirst for knowledge, and she was content with the answer she got; at least for now.

"Tomorrow, a new chieftain will be chosen." Rika was silent for a moment. "You would make a great leader for us."

Vierra laughed, dryly and coldly, as was her style. "You know very well that Aure will be chosen. That is what her mother has prepared her for. She cared for nothing else." Vierra's expression turned grim.

Rika opened her mouth to say something but decided against it and turned to lie down on her back. It wasn't long until Rika's even breathing joined Launi's heavier snore.

Vierra could not get off to sleep, even though the day had been strenuous. She added firewood to the hut's fireplace one more time. The embers would keep them nice and warm into the long hours of the morning. Her speeding thoughts wandered from Aure and the dead chieftain, to the lean-to in the forest, and to the new and mysterious inhabitant within it. The night passed slowly, and finally Vierra dozed off in the morning hours, borne by restless dreams of blue-eyed men, black blades, and dark-haired persecutors.

Despite being very tired, Vierra left the camp as soon as the first ray of light was visible in the eastern sky. Others were still deep in slumber, and even the dogs were not aware of her movements when she sneaked to the dark forest. She brought with her a big serving of dry fish and some cooked deer meat from last week's hunt. Vierra stepped through the forest as fast as she could.

The morning unraveled, cold and clear. There was a thick layer of frost everywhere; the rain of the last few days had frozen on the ground and rimed the trees. Here and there were leaves, still bright in color, but most of them had changed now to a brown, even mass. Even the evergreen conifers looked bleak in the cold light of the autumn sun. On the northern horizon, there was a dark, ominous front of clouds, which slowly moved closer as the morning went on.

Arriving at the lean-to, Vierra saw the fire still burning joyfully. She realized she was relieved at seeing Vaaja in good strength, building up the fire.

"Vi-er-ra, Vi-er-ra." The man tried to pronounce her name when she arrived. Vierra dropped her burdens beside the lean-to, and a smile forced its way onto her tired face.

"Let's see your leg. After that, I must go immediately. The chieftain is dead and I have to bid farewell. You will do nicely with this food." Vierra knew that the man might not have understood what she said, but nonetheless she felt that she had to give a reason for her departure.

"Chieftain, big chieftain-man," the man tried. It seemed that chieftain, as a word, was familiar to him.

Vierra laughed wholeheartedly, something she hadn't done for a long time. "The chieftain is not a man. She is a woman. Wouldn't that be odd, a man as a leader? Now, let us look at the wound and get you some more firewood."

While working on the wound, Vierra tried to figure out why she didn't grieve the old chieftain's death. She didn't hate her foster mother, not really. She had taken Vierra under her wing and done her duty. She had, however, given all her strength and energy to Aure, whom she wanted to be the tribe's next chieftain. After passing to adulthood, Vierra hadn't wanted to compete for the attention.

The hurried chores disrupted her brooding thoughts and forced her to focus on the job at hand. Vaaja's injury had started to heal well and the skin around it was only slightly red. Vierra washed the plant wrapping away and replaced it with a new one. She chopped more firewood from the dead tree she had found the day before and, with a wave to Vaaja, she hurried back to join the ceremony with the rest of the tribe.

In the insipid dawn light, the Seita stone glowed reddish-brown, as if foreshadowing the scene that would soon follow. The stone was human-shaped and human-sized. It leaned toward the east, as if bowing to the rising sun. For some reason, no trees grew around it; there was just a circle-shaped area covered with an even carpet of moss. The tribe members silently arrived one after another from the forest. First came Aure, accompanied by two men who were carrying her mother on an ornate bier. Behind them walked Eera. The night's effort had exhausted her and as she walked, she leaned on her red-haired apprentice, Rika.

Behind them came the rest of the tribe with their children. Vierra was among the last. She had made it back from her early trip in the morning, but only after a brisk run through the forest. Every tribe member had firewood with them. Small children just had one branch, but men and women carried hefty armfuls. They approached the Seita stone and placed the wood on the ground, piece by piece. An even pile of wood formed near the stone, and the chieftain was placed on top of it, on her pallet. She was clothed in her best deerskin, and on her arms and face were painted beautiful, spiral-shaped patterns. Graceful was the leader in her dying dress, even though she had been old and sick. The torch that Rika had in her other hand was given to Aure, and she lit it using her tinderbox. Made of wood, skin greased in deer fat, and dry grass, the torch lit easily and burned with a large flame which fluttered in the wind.

Eera sang with a clear voice as Aure lit the pyre from different spots with the torch:

> *Fade away in Kainu heartland*
> *Pretty is the day to die*
> *Beautiful to burn to ashes*
> *Windy air with whom to fly*
>
> *Start the fires down below*
> *Keep your torches lighted*
> *Guide your daughters, guide your sisters*
> *Keep us all united*
>
> *Until the last day will arrive*
> *Setting of the final sun*
> *All of Kainu then are with you*
> *All of Kainu's work is done*

The dry wood started to burn, and the pyre flamed up high, driven by the strong northern wind. The old features of the chieftain melted in the fire, and a strong stench of burning flesh was released into the air.

"The smell of the netherworld," Eera confirmed.

Nobody cried. The chieftain had been a tenacious woman when alive and in the celebration of death, she had to be honored the same way. If Rika, an emotional girl, had been on the pyre instead of the chieftain, everyone would be crying and sobbing, in keeping with her nature. Slowly, the wood burned away, and the leader in the middle diminished until only charred remains were left. Eera smelled the flames and grunted approvingly. The stinging smell of death had evened out; now was the time for burial.

The men of the tribe dug a shallow hole through the moss just beside the Seita stone. When they had finished, they lowered the charred remains of the chieftain into the hole. Atop her, they placed two iron-tipped spears, crossed, and a bear's skull: the marks of a chieftain. They filled the hole until it was even again and stomped it well.

"This is the chieftain's stone now. Here, we can come for luck and advice, all of us who helped to ease her journey." Eera's face showed relief – one great deed done, the other still ahead.

"The leader has fallen, long live the tribe. A new chieftain on top of the old one!" Eera yelled, so loudly that the meadow blared. "Aure, the chieftain's daughter, she is strong. Two husbands. She should be the new leader!" Eera presented her candidate in the traditional way, yelling energetically.

"Vierra is better, the one called Fargoer! Best hunter, best tracker, best woman with a bow." Rika introduced the rival. Vierra looked at her friend. *I wish I had her faith*, she thought.

Silence fell over the field. Eera continued:

"Because there are no other candidates, the rocks shall decide. Those who are for Aure, put a white stone in the jar. Those for Vierra, a dark one." One of the tribe members had brought a gathering jar with her. It was a clay jar of fine craftsmanship, with a narrow mouth. During gatherings, all adults always had two stones with them, a white one and a dark one. Now everyone, when his or her turn came, dropped one stone in the jar, either a dark or a white one depending on which candidate was more to his or her liking.

When everyone had dropped their stones, Eera took the jar and held it high over her head. She poured the rocks out near the Seita stone, onto the even, mossy surface. Just a few dark stones fell down among the white ones. There were many rocks on the ground. In Eera's youth, only women could carry gathering rocks, even though men and children could participate by attending the gathering. These days, men were considered equals and could vote, and male witches had even been seen in the winter camps, singing songs. However, the role of the chieftain was still always held by a woman.

"The rocks have spoken, Aure is the new leader of our tribe." From some stash inside her garb, Eera dug out a necklace made of bear claws. She had taken it from the old chieftain's neck during her session with the dead. Slowly, she strung it around Aure's neck. It would not be removed as long as Aure ruled. The tribe, as one, let out a primal cheer, as much for the luck of the new chieftain as to drive away evil spirits. Aure's sad, tired face turned stern as she started to speak. Now was the moment for which she had prepared for so long.

Vierra looked at her cousin, who was enjoying this brief moment in time. She had often wondered what life would be like after Aure became the chieftain. Now, in that instant, she saw Aure in front of her as the same Aure as always. The chieftain's sash wouldn't change anything between them.

"Today, we get ready for the deer hunt that is coming soon. We will gather our supplies and send the scouts –"

Aure's first speech as the leader was cut short by a murmur that started in the crowd. "A Turyan, on holy ground! Turyan, go away!" was echoing from the people's mouths. And it was true. A black-haired Turyan man stepped into the middle of the meadow. His shoulder was in a thick bandage, and his dark, stinging eyes searched until they found Vierra in the crowd.

"You have invaded sacred ground, Turyan. You would not stand there, lest I dishonored the peace of the gathering. Flee while you still can." Aure's challenge was strong in the air: fresh power from the new leader.

"Honored chieftain. I approach your gathering with neither wily nor evil thoughts. I have come for justice. Is that not the purpose of this thing?" The Turyan spoke the tribe's language with a heavy accent, but his words were clear.

"He is right. The old laws say that anyone can come to the gathering to make demands, if he subjects them to the tribe's will. The gathering-peace concerns others than the Kainu, so long as they respect it by behaving correctly," said Eera.

Aure nodded to confirm the words of her elder. The expression on her face revealed a mind filled with uncertainty.

"Fine. My name is Tuura, and my demand is for that woman." The Turyan pointed his finger at Vierra. "Yesterday, she interfered with a matter that does not concern her: the punishment of a thieving slave. She also wounded me with an arrow." The man revealed his shoulder beneath the bandage. It had an ugly, ragged wound in it. An ordinary man wouldn't be standing with a wound like that, but this one did not seem to mind or care.

"Do you deny this, Vierra? Is he a liar, or did this really happen?" asked Eera. Everyone's eyes turned to Vierra, who looked uneasy. At last she spoke.

"It happened like he said. He tried to kill the man, and I stopped him. I could have shot into the heart instead of the shoulder." There were sighs from the tribe in the air and then a deep silence. Even the children were quiet, sensing the tension.

"Where is this man now?" asked Eera, seemingly untouched by the surprise.

"Hiding in a place where this Tuura's knife cannot reach him," Vierra said. "His name is Vaaja, and he does not deserve to be butchered like a squirrel."

"He must be brought here. If two people fight, often a third one can uncover the truth," Eera answered.

"He is wounded and cannot walk this far and he does not speak our language."

"Aure's men will go and help. They will make sure that he doesn't escape and will help him get here." Eera had instinctively taken the role of speaker, even though it belonged to Aure by status. People in the gathering seemed not to notice, as they were preoccupied by the drama unfolding before them.

"I will go, too," said Tuura.

"You will go nowhere until the matter has been settled. If you really tried to kill this man, you will not be given a chance to do so until it's proven that you have a right to do it. If you try, a dozen of our hunters will come after you, and they will not set their aim for your shoulder."

"You shall do as the gathering orders. You did bring your issue to us, so you will obey," confirmed Aure bluntly.

Tuura sat down with a sour look on his face. Vierra and the men started off: the gathering's command was holy and had to be followed immediately.

The sun rose higher, melting the white frost into a glimmering dew on the bare branches of the trees and the yellow grass. From the north, a mass of clouds rolled and enveloped the sun, stealing away its glimmer. The journey to the lean-to was like a nightmare in bright daylight. Aure's formidable men walked by her sides in silence, like robust shadows. Vierra's mouth didn't open either, but her mind pushed out thoughts one after another until they tripped over each other and fell down. No thought could grant her an escape, and time passed by faster than she would ever have wanted. They quickly arrived at the lean-to Vierra had constructed, and at the man sheltering inside it.

Vierra would never forget Vaaja's face as it was when they met at that moment. His friendly and open gaze turned first into puzzlement, and then to hurt and despair.

"Don't worry, it will be fine. I will defend you in the gathering. All will turn out for the best." Vierra's words tried to soothe, but her voice told a story of uncertainty and fear.

Vaaja didn't answer. He either didn't understand or didn't want to. Aure's men indicated for him to start moving, and Vaaja got up, dragging his wounded leg clumsily. Vierra went beside him, intending to help, but he pushed her away and walked arduously through the forest on his own, guided by Aure's men.

The journey through the woods was rough for the wounded man, and their progress slowed down as he grew more tired, constantly falling down headlong. The surrounding landscape became hostile as well, and threw down a cold rain on the struggling wanderers.

Vierra's heart ached as she saw how Vaaja fell down time and time again. Each time, it took longer for him to get up, but he accepted no help and always got up on his own. Aure's men seemed to instinctively understand his will because they didn't even try to help. Vierra didn't share their insight and tried to help every time – and was turned down again and again. The arrow wound in Vaaja's leg opened up again and blood spilled from it, staining his pant leg dark – as dark as the mind of the woman who was walking behind him.

The painstaking journey finally ended, and four travelers stepped into an opening in front of the drenched people in the gathering. Nobody was allowed to leave the gathering spot before all the issues had been resolved. "Cold and hunger often drive past the argument," the old ones used to say. So once again, no member of the tribe had had any food or drink. Breast-fed children were the only ones who got something to eat during the wait. And when the rain had set upon them, there was no shelter or permission to leave.

Vaaja fell prone at the opening, taking a deep breath. With a huge effort, he struggled to his feet and, with his head held high, he stared at the black-haired Tuura. Despite his seeming courage, his bleak gaze was one of a trapped animal. Eera did not wait, but started the hearing. Water dripped from her gray hair, but her determination did not falter.

"Is your name Vaaja, and are you the slave of this Turyan, called Tuura?"

"Vaaja," the man said and tapped himself on the chest. "Vaaja slave." After this, he spoke in his own tongue. Eera replied to him occasionally, using the same language, although roughly spoken, and Vaaja continued his flood of words for a moment.

Then Eera turned to the others.

"The language of the Bjarmia. I have heard it before and understand it a little. He tells me he was a Bjarmian trader, whom Tuura captured and gave to his master, a Turyan witch, as a gift. From there, he escaped, stealing from the witch's supplies to do so. Tuura, what did this slave steal? What do you need to return to your master?"

"That belt he is wearing," Tuura said, pointing at the fair-skinned man.

"Take the belt off him, we will see it." Aure's strong men took the belt from Vaaja's waist and held it high up in the air so everyone could see. It was pitch-black leather and ornamented with small white bones.

"The belt of death. The belt of a witch. Made of leather from a sea monster, the kind that dwell in the far north. Finger-bones of witches are attached to it, fingers of great witches, indeed. Two days that slave-dog escaped me with its help, with an arrow in his skin, until even the belt didn't give him strength anymore. I will get the slave as my reward for the ordeal I have suffered. I have decided that I do not need him, but instead I will kill him as punishment for his theft and escape bid. You can see now that I have committed no violation, and both the belt and the slave can be given to me. The belt, I will deliver to my master. This woman's attack against me was unprovoked, and I demand compensation from her. Fifty squirrel skins, or, if she cannot give them, one moon-cycle of service to me in my lands that are in the far north."

Silence descended over the gathering. Only a lonely wind wailed in the naked trees. The tribe, beaten by rain and chilly weather, waited in silence for Eera's answer. Eera looked thoughtful and finally said:

"This is my proposal. Your demands toward the belt Vaaja carries are just, and you will have it. Vaaja you can also have, because he is an outsider, not because he was a slave. We have no slaves, and his slavery is not relevant to the gathering. Vierra you will not get, as those who go to the Turyan land never return. We will, together, deliver you ten squirrel skins, and then you will be on your way, content with the skins, Vaaja, and the belt. Which will it be? White stone shall stand for my proposal, and black yours."

Vierra's worst fear was about to come true, and she intervened for the first time after arriving at the glade.

"Is this how we treat peaceful people who walk our lands? Do we let the Turyan arbitrariness prevail? The old chieftain wouldn't have accepted this. What do you think, Aure?" Vierra turned her pleading gaze toward her cousin, who had stood still during the whole incident. Aure looked instinctively to Eera, searching for support.

"The law is the law, and we cannot cease to follow it even if we wanted to," Eera replied, as if sensing Aure's question, which came without words.

Aure twisted her hands as the choice was ripping her into two directions. "What can I do, Vierra? You heard what Eera said."

Vierra's face froze into a grim expression, and she didn't say another word.

After the decision, the gathering rocks rolled in and out from the jar, but not a single black rock landed on the moss.

Without hesitation, Vierra walked to Vaaja, who was standing slumped in the rain, and gave him a long kiss on the lips. "So I take you, Vaaja of the Bjarmia, as my man. Breed me to give girls and bring fish from the sea, and you shall live happily until the day I die. Will you accept?"

Everyone was holding their breath as they waited for Vaaja's answer. The man was shocked senseless by all that was happening and could not say a word. It seemed that he barely understood what the woman was asking of him. Tuura's wits, however, came around, and he realized what was about to happen.

"Kainu wench, it will be hard to marry a dead man!"

As he was shouting, he drew his hooked blade from his belt and surged towards the unarmed Vaaja, his obvious intention being to surprise and kill the man on the spot before anyone could react.

Fast was the black blade of the Turyan, swooping at Vaaja's unprotected throat. Luckily for Vaaja, this was not the first time he had seen a knife-blade and, even though he was wounded, he dodged the incoming blow. He grabbed Tuura by the knife arm, and they started to struggle for control.

Hardened by countless battles, Tuura was an overwhelming opponent for the wounded youngster. He kicked Vaaja in the injured leg, causing him to fall onto the moss and writhe in agony. The Turyan raised his weapon high in the air in order to finish the job with one strong thrust. But the death strike never found its mark. A kick to the back of his knee felled him before his knife could land on his prey. As he turned, Tuura saw Vierra. She stood there holding a scramasax, a nearly arm-length knife. It was a beautiful weapon and common among the warriors of her tribe. Water was pouring down her black hair, and her green eyes emanated dark conviction.

Tuura instinctively directed his attention toward this new opponent. They started circling each other, looking for weaknesses. The Kainu gave way, and soon there was an arena around them, its edges made of people. A duel was, although rare, a completely acceptable way to solve conflicts permanently. The Turyan was a fierce knife fighter, but he had been wounded by the arrow in the shoulder and because of that, wielded his knife with his left hand. Vierra was rather inexperienced, but compensated with the ferocity of youth and determination of heart. They circled and circled, feinting attacks and rousing each other.

"Turyan mutt, go home with your tail between your legs!"

"Wench! Because of you, I will kill him slowly. His fate will be yours to thank for!"

"Over my dead body, you witch's dog!"

Like this and in a dozen other ways, they mocked each other. Vierra's knife slowly started to find openings in the Turyan's defense. Once, then a second time, Vierra's knife struck, drawing blood from her opponent's arms and upper body. Then, after Vierra yet again wounded him, he suddenly lashed out with his arrow-wounded right arm. The arm described a large arc towards her and, as Vierra was unprepared for this kind of attack, it hit her face with tremendous strength. The woman was thrown back by the force of the blow like a ragdoll and was left lying in the moss, blood spurting from her mouth and nose.

Vierra felt two forces fighting inside her. The first one urged her to give way to the darkness that pulsed on the edge of her tortured mind, ready to sink her into the merciful embrace of unconsciousness. Then she would know nothing and wouldn't have to determine the oncoming fate of this young man. It didn't concern her, anyway.

There was another voice, though. It was the voice of a gray she-wolf, who looked at Vierra with her yellow eyes and yelled, "Fight! Are you so weak, a quitter? Did Mother really waste words with you in our people's cave? Coward!"

Lightning-fast, Tuura turned and rushed his knife towards Vaaja, who was on the edge of the arena. Suddenly, with a soft, cracking sound, the attacking man fell on his face at the feet of his would-be victim. He stayed there, lying motionless on the ground. From the back of his neck stuck out the reddened blade of Vierra's scramasax, which she had thrown.

"Over my dead body, like I said." Vierra fell back to the wet moss, unconscious.

The deer had gathered in large herds. Before the arrival of the heavy blankets of snow, they would leave for their winter lands. Small tribes of Kainu were gathered together as well. The large deer hunt would provide everyone with food for long into the winter. Lingonberries were gathered, and small, round-cheeked children ate them till their stomachs were sore. Men and women met in deer and lingonberry feasts, and in the spring there would once again be fewer people living in the huts for lone men and women.

Even though there were no flowers for the autumn wedding, the celebration was still grand. After scrubbing each other in the sweat hut, the couple had been crowned with twig wreaths made by children of the tribe. Twigs were also plentiful in the feasting place and, in a ceremony that Eera held, everyone drank honey mead and ate so much that they could barely move. Vaaja was wearing his black belt, which was, according to the tribe's laws, now his until someone came to the gathering to demand it.

The eyes of the cousins were evading each other during the festivities. Nevertheless, they both had their reasons to be happy during that autumn day. Aure was the chieftain now and would soon lead the tribe to the winter camp in her mother's footsteps. Vierra had a husband now, and with him the years of loneliness would be left behind for good.

Of Fire and Stone

Fire

THE MIDSUMMER river presented a beautiful and ever-changing view for the travelers in the majestic long-boat. The sun smiled down on the rowers, and in the blue sky sailed just a few white strips of clouds. The river was wide at that spot, so wide that a grown man couldn't have thrown a rock from the shore even halfway across. The longboat was like a sight from another world in this peaceful scenery, and it was indeed far from its homeport.

The boat was larger than any of the Kainu's fishing boats, and it made the water foam grandly as it glided slowly up the river. The rowers were longhaired and bearded, sturdy men, each with an oar in hand. Those oars they pulled slowly, forcing the longboat to travel sluggishly upstream. Many of them eyed the surrounding forest suspiciously. These men had crossed the sea and were far away from their homes.

On the bow of the boat stood a stunted old man. He created a completely different image with his dark, thin hair, crooked back, and bowlegs. They were on his business, though, and the silver he had promised was the force that had taken the longboat this far. And truly, he was guiding the boat like a bloodhound sniffing the wind, his large, crooked nose turned upwards.

Upstream, far away from the eyes of the longboat-men, a much plainer vessel was traversing the river. The boat was narrow and unsteady, like riverboats tended to be, but it carried its three passengers evenly and without complaint.

Vaaja sat at the oars, in good strength and with a smile on his face. Vierra was steering from the back and looking at her husband while she adjusted her black hair, with her free hand. Her green eyes glowed and her mind wandered free as a summer bird. She thought back to the time when Vaaja had arrived from the north, an arrow in his leg and a pursuer at his back. How this stranger's life had intertwined with her own, lonely one. So tightly were they bound that she couldn't see how they could ever be separated again.

Coming from a trader's family, Vaaja had quickly learned Vierra's language. He was from Bjarmia, a country that lay far in the east on the shores of the vast northern sea. As natural traders, they sold the harvest of the cold sea to go with the Vikings and Bolgars all the way to the far lands of the unknown south. Vaaja had been there, too, many times with his father. Often, while he and Vierra were lying beside their evening fire in each other's arms, Vaaja had told many amazing stories of these journeys. Of southern lands, huge cities lying behind great rivers, pathless passages, and of their riches. Vaaja's tales meandered further, to the far ends of the world. There, glamorous cities rose straight up from yellow deserts and women walked on paved roads, their faces concealed. So rich and powerful were the rulers of the cities that even their slave women carried silver jewelry around their necks.

Vierra listened to Vaaja's stories often and with pleasure, but the longing in her heart was finally quenched. The blond-haired man had brought her peace, and she missed nothing. The memories of the First Mother were far, far away. Just distant ramblings, undoubtedly only apparitions of her own vivid imagination.

If the man from Bjarmia had tamed Vierra, the boy that sat in the middle bench had cast a final, unbreakable bond on her. Vierra's face melted into a rich smile as she looked at her son. His face was round and framed by yellow, stubborn wisps of hair. The hair and the blue eyes the boy had inherited from his father, who rowed the boat. The boy, who carried the name Vaalo, had seen five summers and had a curiosity that knew no boundaries. Even now, he was reaching over the boat's edge, allowing the cool waters of early summer to flow through his small hand. He sometimes rolled over the edge in his enthusiasm, to be saved by his father or mother. Every day with the boy was full of happiness, of joy, of temper, and of all the little things their lives had to give. And Vierra needed nothing else.

Vierra forgot the steering as she watched the boy, and they almost ran aground. At the last moment, she snapped to attention and steered the boat clear. Vierra smiled because Vaaja did not even notice. Even though he had learned to survive in the wilderness during their years together, he was still a born trader and a townsman. So, naturally, he left the responsibility to Vierra as they traveled together in the wilds.

It was the eve of the fire festival, the day when the sun would be at its highest point and would start the slow descent towards the winter darkness. The old ones said that the fire festival was a custom of the southern peoples. Nonetheless, it had been celebrated by the Kainu for years. It was customary to find a beautiful spot for the occasion, where the people would then gather in numbers to feast and burn a pyre. This was their plan, too, and the boat moved rapidly, taking the trio towards the festival site they had chosen. Birds were chirping in the thickets surrounding the river, working as a choir for their celebration.

Vierra and Vaaja often spent time by themselves in the summers, and then with their son after he was born. At first, they had been scared of a party coming from the north to seek revenge, but the northern forest had kept its demands. They had burned and buried Tuura appropriately; there was no reason to irritate the spirit of such a powerful man. Vierra had defeated him in an honest fight at the gathering, so in the eyes of the tribe she had committed no violation.

What started as caution soon turned into a way of life. Accordingly, Vierra didn't want to participate in her tribe's fire festival, and they had found their own place for the celebration. Earlier that morning, they had fished and the river had indeed given them a good amount of trout for the feast. In the caressing light of the sun, the celebration site struck them with its beauty. On the shore of a small lake that rested below roaring rapids spread a small, forest-bordered glade. The short but bright summer of the north had cast a breathtaking field of flowery brilliance all over the clearing. They ran their boat ashore, and Vaaja gathered firewood for the pyre with their son. Vierra cleaned the fine catch of trout that they had caught. They would prepare them later, slowly, in the warm glow of the fire.

Before lighting the bonfire, Vierra had one more task to complete. If the fire festival was originally a southern tradition, the ritual hunt was an ancient, sacred thing for the Kainu. The head of the family was supposed to hunt alone before the brightest night of the summer. The luck they would have for hunting and fishing over the next year could be divined from the hunt's results.

Into Vierra's mind flashed a memory of the evening before; of how she and Vaaja had drowsily listened to their son's even breaths as they lay in each other's arms, quietly talking by the deep-red light of the hut fire.

"You're not seriously going to hunt alone tomorrow?" Vaaja had said, fondling Vierra's shiny, dark hair.

"Of course I am," Vierra had answered, maybe too sharply, as the boy had started to turn restlessly in his sleep. He calmed down a moment afterwards and went back to sleep.

"Why do you want to go? You didn't want to celebrate with the others. I thought you didn't care about the old ones' traditions."

"The fire festival has nothing to do with it. Don't you realize what happiness we have gotten for ourselves?" Vierra had looked at her sleeping son and then turned her gaze back to her husband's blue eyes.

"Even the forest has given to us in abundance. There's no hunger, no thirst. Have we given thanks for it?"

"You always offer part of the bounty to the dwellers of the earth, and sometimes blood, too. And we haven't had that much luck. I'd like more sons." Vaaja had glanced at their son, who was fast asleep.

"Is there something wrong with that one?" Vierra hadn't even tried to cover her hurt tone. "The people of the earth will give you their blessings for a moment, but the great spirits will grant a lasting happiness. I will hunt and speak with them when I bring back the catch. And we should have more girls, not boys."

"But–" Vaaja had started. Vierra silenced her husband by kissing him. Their talking was done for the time being, and they had both gone to sleep, each with their own thoughts.

As Vierra gathered her bow and arrows, her mind full of memories, Vaaja returned from gathering firewood.

"If you go for the hunt, at least take the Turyan belt with you for luck," Vaaja said, removing the dark belt from his slender hips.

"You know I don't like it. It feels cold and unfamiliar to carry. Besides, I have hunted alone countless times and never before have I needed Turyan luck to succeed."

"Take it this time in honor of the fire festival. I have no need for it here in the ceremony field."

Vierra was about to resist but, surprising herself, she bent to her husband's will.

"So be it. At least I will return faster with the Turyan luck in my footsteps."

They embraced for a long time, and the matter was settled. When they argued, they could not stay angry with each other for long, but naturally came to an agreement quickly.

Vaaja had become a good Kainu man, Vierra thought with a smile. Her sisters in the tribe had at first suspected that he would be nothing more than a burden and a nuisance, and at first he had indeed been unable to do anything useful. He couldn't hunt, he couldn't fish, and of traps he knew even less. It was decided that he couldn't be let into the woods alone, either, after Vierra had rescued him from being lost forest a few times. But Vaaja was tenacious and ductile, a patient learner, and so he soon started to be successful in his undertakings. Being a tall man, he never grew very stealthy, so he was a rather clumsy hunter. He was very good with boats, though; as a trader, he had traveled and spent a lot of time offshore. Fishing became one of his favorite chores. It was he who had caught most of the trout that sunny morning.

Whereas Vierra and Vaaja did not have any discord between them, disputes with the boy were another matter entirely. Vaalo did not really mind hunting, as long as he could come, too. When he heard that was not going to happen, he would immediately fly into a rage and refuse to speak to his parents.

Vierra let her green eyes rest on the beautiful setting one more time before departing. Vaaja, who was piling the last pieces of wood on the pyre, smiled. The wind blew his light hair as he waved goodbye. Vaalo was sitting in the center of the glade, arms crossed, inexorable offense on his face. He looked at his smiling mother from under his brow and refused to wave. Vierra walked to him and ruffled her stubborn son's hair. It took more than this to console him, though and, with a sigh, Vierra finally started toward the edge of the forest. She gazed at the sulking, round-faced rascal until the trees on the edge of the glade obstructed the view. For a moment, Vierra felt a strong urge to go back and forget about the whole hunt. Why not just stay there with Vaaja and Vaalo, to burn the fire and eat trout? She dismissed the thought, however, and continued further into the forest.

Stone

The floor of the forest was cool and calm. The hot sunlight sifted down from in between the leaves and twigs and did not burn with its full strength. Hunter's instincts took over the lone woman, and she, for a moment, forgot the glade and her family that was waiting there. She heard, saw, and smelled, she mingled with the forest's shadows, became one of its mysterious travelers. It had been like this for her people since the time of her ancestors, a long time ago. There was just the forest, the hunter, and the prey.

Vierra did not have a clear thought about where to go, since mid-summer was not the most favorable time for hunting. The big game was spread out, and smaller animals did not leave tracks as they did in the wintertime snow. Summer was a time for fishing, not hunting, for the Kainu, and often they came back from the ritual hunt empty-handed. Vierra let her instincts guide her on where to go.

A jaybird, the hunter's friend, flew onto a branch next to Vierra and looked at her with its dark eyes. Its beak turned busily from one side to another as it watched the woman's actions curiously. Seeing a jaybird always brought back memories from a particular summer years ago. The weather had been very similar to today, warm and bright. Vierra could still hear her mother Asla's voice in her mind as she taught her the hunters' ways.

Asla had been a skilled hunter, even though many had thought she should have been the witch's apprentice. It was true that she saw visions and omens, and often she was seen staring into nothingness with a sad look on her face. She had also only taken one man, which was considered odd. Nevertheless, she was the chieftain's sister and an able woman in her affairs. It was considered even stranger that, after her husband died, she didn't take a new man to help her care for her little girl, Vierra.

Awakening from her memories, Vierra finally ended up wandering towards a low hill. Its top, bare save for a few trees, loomed as a land-mark from afar. When approaching it, she noticed faint deer tracks that headed up to the top of the hill. Vierra knew the deer were up there for a reason. The wind would carry away the insects that were harassing them and give them a moment of relief.

Vierra considered her point of approach for a moment. Obviously she had to stay downwind of them, otherwise the summer breeze would carry her scent to the deer and expose her. She also had to be aware of boulders and small rocks, as dislodging one of those would scare the whole herd away, scattering them everywhere in the forest.

Slowly and carefully, she moved forward, one sneaky step at a time, toward the animals.

It was deer that Vierra had hunted with her mother on their last hunting trip as well. Even though Vierra had scared them away with her clumsiness, her mother had not been angry. She just laughed at her blundering. Maybe she had seen beforehand that she was together with her child for the last time.

Vierra angrily drove away the memory of her mother's death. She wanted to remember her as she was when they hunted together: brave, beautiful, mysterious, standing on the top of a hill, looking into the distance. And it didn't matter anymore – not now that she had Vaaja and Vaalo. They filled every day of her life.

From between the trees, she saw one big and three small deer. From this small herd Vierra chose a fawn, which was scrabbling for withered grass in between the rocks near its mother, its keen nostrils twitching as they sniffed the wind. The fawn instinctively tried to stay near the safety of her mother, and Vierra waited for the moment that they would separate, even for a second. She cocked an arrow on the bow-string and slowly, as if in a dream, drew it back near her ear. So good was she with a bow that they didn't allow her to participate in the winter camp shooting competitions. Sometimes Vierra even closed her eyes and shot instinctively. Often, she felt a close relationship with the arrow, as if it were part of herself, an extension of her hunting will. She had considered telling Eera about this, but had decided not to bother the witch with a matter that only brought her joy and good hunting. Even the bows had to have their own spirits, and she just happened to be in their favor.

Her instincts brought her luck once again, and the arrow reached its goal unerringly. The young animal fell on the spot, and the rest of its kind escaped the hill, scattering with the speed of the wind. Vierra ran to her catch and twisted the young animal's neck with all her strength until she felt it give away under her knee. After that, she cut open the fawn's neck artery. As the bright red blood flowed to the rocky ground, she spoke her words of thanks to Mielikki, the mistress of the forest.

> *Mielikki, mother of forest*
> *Take this offering of blood*
> *Dripping in your holy ground*
> *Luck and game for me let flood*
>
> *Mielikki, please give me prey*
> *Let not your servant starve*
> *Bring your hunter broader pack*
> *Let me thrive, my fortune carve*

After the words had faded away, Vierra opened the deer's stomach, took out its gall bladder and poured the bitter fluid on top of the blood that had soaked into the ground.

> *Tapio, ruler of the forest*
> *Catcher of the strongest gall*
> *Grant for me now the largest game*
> *Fill my stock now for the fall*

Once the holy words had been spoken and the sacrifice made, Vierra lifted the carcass onto her shoulders and started her journey back to the glade. In her mind, she was rejoicing; rarely did a ritual hunt succeed this well. There was plenty of time left in the day for celebration, and fawn meat would join the trout in the fire.

Vierra made straight for the glade. After a short trek, she arrived at a small opening in the forest that was covered in large rocks. Here and there between the rocks grew long patches of grass and a few withered trees, their fragile branches waving in the light wind. Black-gray adders were bathing on the rocks in the sun, hissing at each other. Vierra was just getting ready to go around the glade when she saw something move across the opening. It was a small, hunchbacked man. His green clothes were like hanging lichen covering his withered and skinny body. He was astonishingly agile, though, jumping from rock to rock, and when he came closer, Vierra saw his crooked shoes hitting the rocks, and blue will o' the wisps and sparks flew in the air. No adder would bite him, even though he ran over them as if completely mindless of them.

The man ran straight towards Vierra, crying from far away: "Vierra, Vierra, why were you so hasty and why did you not give the proper sacrifice to the Seita?"

"What Seita?" Vierra had always honored her ancestors' holy places, even though her sacrifices and prayers were often directed to the new gods, as was the custom these days. She wondered how the man could know her name. She'd had no time to tell him, and she had never seen him before.

"The Seita who lives on the top of the hill. It was malicious and bitter even when I was floating helpless in my mother's womb."

"I saw no Seita," Vierra defended herself. She was annoyed by this strange and truculent man, but she kept a polite tone towards her elder.

"You didn't even try. You were only thinking of Mielikki and Tapio, you wench, while you were drawing the gall bladder to Seita's rocky side. They were the ones who took the gall from under Seita's rocky nose. Those bastards are southern gods, of those who root the earth and bite hay. Pthew!" The old man projected a long wad of spittle from between his bony jaws.

Vierra was dumbfounded by the outburst of this complete stranger. As he babbled, he walked closer, causing Vierra to flinch and take a step back. He smelled bad, of stale urine, and of unknown, deep earth and forest.

"Seita will have her revenge and so will I. Whose belt have you around you? My belt. Give it to me and bow before me for mercy, and I might forgive you."

Vierra's spirit flared up. Who did this man think he was? That kind of behavior went beyond all understanding and, even though he was older, it was inappropriate for a man to speak thus to a woman.

"The belt is not mine but my husband's, so I cannot give it to you. And I am not responsible to you for my doings. My chieftain is a woman and so was my mother and my mother's mother. Go away and leave me alone."

The man stared at Vierra along his large nose. "We shall see about belts and mercy."

He let out a cackling laugh and started running surprisingly fast through the rocky glade, disappearing into the forest on the opposite side.

Vierra stared after him and tried to figure out what had just happened. After he had vanished into the forest, Vierra continued her journey. Dark thoughts rose up from her mind, one after another, bothering her travel and making her instinctively speed up her pace.

Blood

Vierra had seen longboats many times before. This one, however, burned itself into her mind forever as she caught sight of it from the hilltop. The proud-bowed vessel had been pulled to the shore of the festival glade, and Vierra felt a hollow, strangling feeling churning in the pit of her stomach. Those wayfarers had many names: persecutors, the tall men, the bearded men, the iron men. Vikings. They came from the west shore of the sea with their longboats every spring, bringing iron, salt, cloth, and silver. They were interested in the furry coats of the animals that the Kainu hunted, as well as the fish that they dried.

The Kainu were happy to trade but stayed cautiously in large groups and areas confined by the trading posts. Everyone, even Vikings, honored them, as they were symbols for peace and trade, and slaying another man in their area would mean a curse on the villain and his family for seven generations. In other places, these men did not always pay, but reclaimed their purchase with axes, swords, and the slaughter of the careless. Why they had come this far from the market places, Vierra did not know.

Fear for her loved ones hastened her step toward the glade. Even though she moved as swiftly as she could, her hunter's instinct forced her also to move silently and stealthily in the forest. If the persecutors noticed her, the hunter would immediately become the prey.

Vaaja, as a trader's son, had had dealings with the Vikings in his earlier days. In springtime, he was in his element in the marketplaces, and the Kainu soon sent him to negotiate in other places as well. Vaaja had explained that it was always best to do a fast trade and change the goods immediately after the deal had been closed. If the oppressors had time to drink too much of the beer that was served in the market, they became unpredictable and arrogant. Vaaja even knew scraps of their language and, with this knowledge, the Kainu had made worthwhile deals for many years.

Soon, Vierra's green eyes caught sight of the festival glade from the shade of the forest that surrounded it. The strangers were going back to their ship, and her frantic gaze moved over the clearing, combing the area for her husband and son. She noticed a vague hump on the ground near the edge of the forest. She rushed toward it, crouched on the grass, and every step increased the despair and horror in her mind.

There was a big hump and a smaller one, both with more than one arrow sticking out of them. Vierra turned them over and her world collapsed. There was Vaaja, his yellow hair stained in blood. There would be no more stories from the southern lands. They had been eternally silenced by the persecutors' arrows. There was Vaalo, the childish gaze of his eyes broken. No more would his laughter tinkle, no more would a small hand reach for his mother. No smile would ever come again from that round face.

Vierra did not cry. She couldn't. The blow was too heavy, the cut too deep. In her mind, she saw the face of the First Mother and remembered what she had said. Deviously, the words had started to come true. The Mother's face disappeared, only to be replaced by that of a gray she wolf. The animal growled, and blood flowed from its exposed fangs. Only the anger was left, a dark, destructive anger towards everything. Anger and then death. And now it was fixed on the murderers who were sneaking away. The child-killers, the robbers, the cowards. Vierra rose and the bow turned to her hand like a thought. It obeyed her order eagerly and sent arrow after arrow toward her enemies. Green eyes directed every one of them to their goal with unerring accuracy. And every one of them bit deep into the flesh of the persecutors. The luckier ones took shelter from the deadly rain, behind the rocks of the beach. One of the men gave orders to the others, and they spread out around the glade, closing in on Vierra from behind their wooden shields, moving from one shelter to another, avoiding the arrows that brought them death. Vierra did not even try to hide, she just kept sending arrows on their way. Some hit the shields, but many times she managed to pass them and the wolf inside her was rewarded with a hoarse yell of pain. Finally, the arrows ran out, and Vierra sank down to embrace her dead son for the last time. From her lips came an old lullaby, which she had often used to lull her little son to sleep. The son who would now sleep forever.

The persecutors ran towards the singing woman, sensing that she wouldn't be a danger to them anymore. Just before they reached Vierra, she drew her scramasax, letting out a primal yell. It was full of anger, despair, and disappointment. So ghastly was the yell that the approaching men stopped for a moment, as if hesitating. When the scream died away, Vierra thrust the blade deep into her stomach, expecting to soon see her son and husband on the river of the Underworld. The hot, searing pain convulsed in her stomach but was extinguished by a blow of a club that struck her head, sending her consciousness into a bright sea of stars, from which it fell into an impenetrable, all-engulfing darkness.

She smelled the fresh forest, heard the spring wind whizzing in her ears. Hints of hut smoke that wafted on the wind mingled with the scent of the forest.

The words, "The forest of the Underworld," escaped from Vierra's lips, and she didn't dare open her eyes.

"Yes, my child," a voice boomed in her head. Vierra couldn't tell the direction it was coming from, but with the same certainty she knew it was true, she also knew that it belonged to the Seita, whom she had passed and ignored when she was hunting.

"Apologize for passing me by, sing a song in my honor and I will let you go. Soon, you'll be with your husband and son. Can you smell the smoke already? There they are, cooking fish and waiting for you."

Vierra was ready to answer on the same breath, to weave a song that would release her from the pain. When she opened her mouth, though, her voice didn't do what she wanted. It was the voice of the wolf and it didn't plead, but asked, "What about the First Mother? I am not supposed to end like this."

Friendship faded from the Seita's voice, and its new tone froze Vierra's blood.

"I will not be asked or denied! Beg for mercy, or do you want to return back to the cold world, a broken woman? There, only endless suffering will await you. Soon, you will finish off what you started with your knife, and come back to ask me for passage to your family. And I will laugh at you and send you to the cold Underworld of the men of iron, where gray spirits moan in endless despair. There, nobody will be of your blood or know your songs. Beg and plead now when you still can."

"You were the one that took my son and husband. Toward you I feel only hatred, and I promise that by my own hand, I will never bring myself to you, now or ever! When I finally come, you will apologize and bow before me."

Vierra spat the words from her mouth in a quick flare of fury. They would haunt her for a long time in the following years.

A longboat was moving slowly downriver and towards the ocean. It had done its duty, and the men were relieved to get away from these unfamiliar waters. The old man standing on the bow had a happy expression on his wrinkled face. A leather belt, pitch black and ornamented with white bones, was wrapped around his waist.

The Roots of Evil

A New Dawn

VIERRA LOVED the morning and waited for it. That short moment when she was about to wake up, but the dizziness of sleep prevented her from remembering where she was. That one moment gave her the strength to keep on fighting. The bleak sun of early autumn forced its way in from the crevices of the walls, and Vierra once again awoke to reality. The moment was over.

Lying next to Vierra in the dark, still asleep, were the two who shared her destiny. She was always the first to awaken, together with the dawn. In the early morning gloom, Vierra looked at the faces of the sleepers. Slumber had momentarily stripped them of their masks of pain.

Alf, a skinny young man, was snoring lightly. His protruding teeth and narrow forehead were clearly distinguishable, even in the gloom. He did his chores quietly and without complaint, as did Vierra. And when he didn't work, he minded his own business.

Beside Alf lay the man they called Oder. They had once asked if it was his real name. It wasn't. His skin was as dark as that autumn morning's twilight, which shrouded the scars and bruises covering his face. Oder was from somewhere far away, where the sun scorched the people's skin dark.

Sensitivity to omens was in Vierra's blood. The day before, the sky had darkened suddenly and the brightest day had turned to a dusk similar to evening. A chilly wind had carried whispers, the message of which Vierra didn't want to hear any more than to understand. A shiver went down her spine. The future looked like impenetrable darkness. It was like black water that had stayed still for a long time, but suddenly stirred.

From underneath a bundle of cloth that Vierra used as a pillow, she heard a familiar voice. These days it spoke to her every morning.

"Take me out."

Vierra obeyed. From underneath her sleeping underlay she pulled a long, badly rusted blade.

"Try me."

Vierra tried. She had kept the blade in as good as possible condition. With her thumb she felt the hard, unforgiving edge.

"Shall we do it today?" the blade asked. Its voice had a waiting, anxious tone. "How easily would I cut flesh, draw blood? Set free?"

Vierra didn't say or do anything. When the blade had presented the same question for the first time, she had thrown the weapon away and forgotten it for a few days. Finally, though, she had placed it back under her mattress. From that day on, the decision had been harder and harder to make.

"Tomorrow," she finally sighed and put the knife back under her berth. She had said so yesterday and the day before, actually for as long as she remembered. Her hand was trembling.

Suddenly, the latch of the summer hut slammed open. With unimaginable speed, the two sleeping denizens of the hut woke up and got to their feet, readying themselves for what their minds, torn away from the freedom of sleep, knew was about to happen.

The door flew open and the light of the autumn dawn squeezed into the hut, together with the person who had opened the door. This large man was living his autumn years. His pitch-black hair was streaked with gray stripes that reached his tangled beard. He was handsomely clothed. The darkness of the man's hair and beard was also in his eyes, the true color of which was perhaps only known by gods – and could possibly have been known by Vierra, had she wanted to look into them. It was impossible to tell the man's exact age, but his eyes gave away that he was even older than he seemed.

The man grabbed Oder, who was standing by the door, with both hands and threw him out of the hut. He was immensely strong and the slave, much scrawnier than him, rolled far away before stopping. Arduously, Oder got to his feet as the blackbeard yelled: "Up, dogs, and get to work!"

The master is in a good mood, Vierra thought. *He didn't even kick Oder after he fell.*

Had she been led into their hut in her present condition, Vierra's family would probably not have recognized her. Her already slim figure had wasted so that she was thin as a rake, and the clear gaze of her green eyes had waned to a feverish glow, which blazed amid a messy black bush of hair. She was as quiet and unpredictable as a wolf that has been chained and subdued to do a dog's work.

Almost three years had passed since violence and murder had torn her from her previous life. The Vikings had not killed her, even though she had slain many men with her bow that day. They revered prowess and courage in combat. The Norsemen had sold her into slavery for a good price in their homeland after she had recovered, against the odds, from her self-inflicted stomach wound.

That had been the beginning of a nightmare in which one day after another passed in a purple-gray haze of violence. Anyone who had lived Vierra's life would have soon released themselves from that merciless torment. There were more than enough opportunities for one who eagerly sought the final escape. Only Vierra's primal willpower and the memory of the discussion with the Seita still kept her clinging on to life. She wouldn't give up, at least not yet.

Vierra slipped out of the summer hut to begin her daily chores. Outside, a familiar scene surrounded her. A great longhouse with its smaller side buildings had been erected near the edge of a large glade. A slowly running creek split the glade in the middle, and there was a bridge that connected it to a field. There Vierra, among others, had been taught many lessons about the work of the hay-biters, lessons learned with pain and suffering. Compared to them, the calluses on her hands were hardly noticeable.

In the middle of the glade stood a great oak, the branches of which shaded the house in the morning and guarded the opening behind the creek at night. The tree was older than the house, older than the glade. Over the centuries, its gnarly roots had reached every corner of the clearing. Even in the furthest point of the glade, it was possible to feel a thick, branch-like lump underfoot.

Walking toward the house, Vierra could hear familiar whispering. She looked at the great oak and then at the edge of the forest glade. A cold shiver ran down her spine. The forest on the edges of the clearing was too dense. It reached for the meadow, and every morning Vierra felt as if it was a bit closer than it had been the morning before. Any forest would have been a comforting home for Vierra. Any forest save this one.

There was enough forest around the house for a day's walk in every direction, but no visitors ever came through it. And the master was the only one to leave; a few times a year he left the glade alone, just to return in a couple of days with more slaves, salt and tools. He seemed to have enough silver to buy all of this. Vierra had lived in the house for two years now and when the master had first brought her into the house, there had been five slaves. Now, there were just three left, and only Alf had been there longer than Vierra.

Vierra felt a wave of nausea rising inside her. She tried to contain it with her will but lost, and knelt down to vomit. Only green bile came out; it had been a while since her last meal.

"Blackboy, stay and make sure that Wolfgirl can work soon. She must try the fish traps." There was threat in the master's voice. Vierra knew that if she couldn't work, she would suffer for it soon.

"Can I give her food? She would recover more quickly to work," Oder replied. There was a strong foreign accent in his speech, even more so than in Vierra's.

"So be it, but hurry. We will go and harvest the turnips."

Vierra sighed. The master was indeed in a good mood.

Oder and Vierra shared a simple meal of turnips, fish and birch-leaf beverage. Oder used this opportunity to eat as well. The master kept a close guard over the food, and the slaves didn't get to eat every day.

"You have been nauseous for many mornings," Oder stated, when they were finishing their meal. "Are you ill?"

"No," said Vierra thoughtfully, as she licked the grease off her hands.

Oder looked at her intently for a moment. Her hips were waiting for food in vain, food which would round them up to a healthier measurement.

"You carry a child inside you," Oder said finally, in a whisper. "Children are the gift of God, but I already grieve for its destiny."

Vierra knew it; had known it deep inside her even though she hadn't admitted it to herself. She felt chilled about giving birth to a child in here, amid all the horror. Something would have to happen before it came.

"It is a bitter gift," Vierra finally answered, wiping bile off the front of her ragged woolen coat. They finished their meal quickly, as any further delay would have been followed by punishment.

Outside, the early autumn day had gotten the best of the morning dusk, and they started to walk toward the field with rapid steps. The forest was silent, as always, except for the quiet whispers. Little birds didn't sing in the glade, nor did the animals of the forest make their trails there. Even the domestic animals that the master brought had to be forced to come there, and it took a long time before they got used to their new life.

The walkers crossed the bridge and stepped toward the working men.

"Are you sick?" the master blurted to Vierra as they arrived to the site. "I have no use for you, if you cannot work."

A sudden burst of mutiny struck Vierra, one she hadn't experienced in a long, long time.

"You should be happy, master, because I will give birth to your son soon. He will be your heir and your keeper in your old age." The wording was kind, but Vierra didn't manage to mask the mockery in her voice.

The master wasn't slow-witted. Still, Vierra's straightforward message took away his confidence for a moment. He had the same cure for loss of confidence as for many other problems: violence. The back of his hand landed a heavy blow on Vierra's cheek, throwing her to the ground.

"I will not bring up brats and, if you cannot work, I will drown you in the river with it, too. And from the fall market I will get two stronger slaves to replace you."

Vierra's weak defiance snapped like a twig. The boat that was about to save her from drowning sank back to deep, dark waters.

I will just sit here. Maybe the master will beat me to death, she thought.

As she sat on the ground holding her cheek, Alf switched everyone's attention to the edge of the forest, where he was pointing.

"Look!" he yelled.

A man had stepped out of the forest, staggering into the glade with feeble, unsure steps. The beard and hair of this large man glimmered red in the sun. There was a bear-like softness in his impressive figure, as well as brisk strength in his movement. His clothes were well-made, although worn and torn after his journey through the woods.

Silently, the whole group hurried closer to this strange apparition. Even Vierra got up slowly and trudged after the others. The red-bearded man brought with him a simple truth: if someone could reach the glade through the forest, it was also possible to leave the same way. Such thoughts were not hers, though. The old Vierra would have darted into the woods long ago, whatever threats the forest could raise against her. But years of blows, repression and subjection had driven that Vierra deep into hiding. She couldn't rise up in an instant anymore.

The group of four people met the redbeard, and saw that his clothes were soaked in blood and his face and arms bruised. There was a glassy, burdened look in his eyes.

"All my men dead... need to get back home..." the man slurred, and clearly didn't realize there were people around him.

"I am Bothvar, also known as Blackbeard. Who are you and how did you find my home, hidden in the forest?"

The man didn't react to the master's question at all.

"Wolfgirl will get water and Loosetooth, you drag him into the house. Blackboy, go and get food for the guest – and make sure you don't stay and eat yourself."

The orders were fulfilled without delay. The master himself followed the actions closely and sharply, and let out a malign yell if he thought any of the slaves was working too slowly. Vierra carried out the orders with her head held low and her thoughts grim, as usual. Oder's eyes held a new kind of glow, however and, when the master was looking elsewhere, he secretly glanced towards the edge of the forest. Alf worked in an even, emotionless rhythm, as if the foreigner didn't exist at all.

When everything possible had done for the redbeard, the master took his slaves to the summer hut and latched the door from outside. Confused, they stood and stared at the locked door. It had been quite a while since they were without work and it was still daylight.

The afternoon passed and nobody had anything to say. Oder was the first to break the silence.

"If that red-bearded man could get here, we can get out. I, for one, am going to try." Oder's growing desire to escape didn't encourage the other two who shared his fate, however.

"Breaking the door will rouse the master's attention," Vierra replied.

Alf seemed distressed. The strange situation confused his mind which now, after years of abuse, only understood the need to work.

"Stop, stop." He pressed his hands to his ears as if trying to deny what was going on around him.

"Shut up or the master will hear! Should we just sit here and wait, doing nothing? I'm trying my luck, in any case," Oder replied. He fiddled with a cross that he had made from reeds. "May God help me succeed."

A cold breeze blew through Vierra's mind. She had seen too many bad things to have hope. Gods wouldn't bother themselves for their sake. She went to her mattress and took out the rusty knife. The others looked at her, dazed. Vierra had not shown the blade to anyone, and nobody would have even guessed that she might have one hidden. Vierra stepped to the summer hut's door and pushed the long blade through a narrow gap, placing the edge below the latch.

At the same instant, the latch rose up with a clang and the door was wrenched open. Whether it was the knife's own will, or the power of Vierra's instinct, none could tell, but, as the latch opened, the weapon slipped behind her back and vanished under the hem of her shirt, light as a shadow.

The master's dark eyes met those of Vierra that were openly staring back at his, green and unyielding. It took only a moment for Vierra's eyes to lower to the level of the master's shoes, but he didn't fail to notice this. A heavy hand slammed against her face once again, sending her flying to the floor. Vierra bowed her head even lower, but the hand holding the knife behind her back didn't lose its grip.

The master's gaze roved around the group of slaves and met only downcast, dispirited eyes. He had never smiled in their presence, but at that moment he was clearly satisfied.

"Wolfgirl and Blackboy, you will go and offer the guest drink and entertainment. Alf will stay here."

Alf looked almost relieved. The ones who left the hut with the master were sullen, and one of them felt the blade of the knife behind her back.

In The Dusk

Shadows of the day were stretching to their evening length by the time the slaves had completed their assigned chores in the house. Vierra had been amazed by it at first, because, unlike most Viking houses she'd seen, there were exquisite, carved-wood tables and benches, in addition to a normal bunk that was built around the edge of the wall. Here and there, she could also see skillfully crafted ornaments and items which represented men and beasts. The master had not carved them; at least they had never seen him do that.

Bothvar was a fine host and offered his best to the guest by the fireplace. It was peaceful in the house, because the animals were still in their outside shelters for summer. The guest was noticeably rejuvenated from his morning state, and awareness had returned to his brown eyes. The blood on his clothes was mostly not his own, but he didn't want to divulge any details about how it had got there. A large bruise on his head had been covered with a piece of cloth that was wrapped around it.

According to their custom, the men went on to discuss the guest's heritage, and it soon turned out that the man's name was Ambjorn and that the master knew his brother and father from a long time ago.

The master told Oder to fetch more beer, and it was drunk heartily, so that Ambjorn's voice soon became loud and his speech more rakish in tone.

Whereas Ambjorn relaxed, the master became more and more silent, and watched his guest even more closely. Soon, Ambjorn was answering even the most intrusive questions, which probed the depth of the man's soul. Anyone else would have been offended and would have accused the master of breaking his hospitality. Ambjorn did not, but rather unburdened his heart as fast as he could, and soon the master did not need to ask anymore.

"I have carved boats for the king and kept a tight house, so that our whole village flourishes, but do my villagers appreciate that? Or me? They do not, but rather they sing songs in honor of my brother,

Thorleik. He returns from his travels every autumn, often without any notable loot, but still it is the food I provide that he tastes in his mouth all winter. And when the work begins in the spring, he gathers the men and takes the best with him for the whole summer."

"But you have a handsome wife, do you not?" the master broke in.

"Handsome and stern, yes. She does not fiddle with silver, she works from dawn till dusk and keeps the house well. The house, aye, but not me. Her hair is golden and her eyes blue, but she is cold as ice."

Ambjorn sighed and drank from his stein.

"Now I have to go. I still have time to reach my home before dark, if I still have one. I thank you for the hospitality and help, and when I reach home I will send you ten buckets of meat and a cask of beer as a reward. Be thanked three times for all your troubles."

Ambjorn got up, ready to leave, but the master placed a hand on his shoulder.

"If you leave in a hurry you can easily go astray, and it is a short time from evening to night. I will get better beer for us to drink, and maybe you can tell me why you hurry to a home where you are not thanked with song. Wolfgirl!" he ordered.

Vierra rushed on hearing her master's order. She had waited out of sight, as it was not wise to be close to the master any more than was necessary. It was a habit dictated more by the will for survival than fear.

"This woman is skinny and unpredictable, but I have beaten the will out of her with my own hands. If you want, you can have her to warm your bed. I guarantee that she will not be an icy woman, if I so command."

There was mockery in the master's voice and eyes, but Vierra was not touched by it. To her, this would just be another ordeal in a long line of ordeals, and it did not raise any surge of emotion inside her anymore. Even being pregnant did not. Vierra knew that the knife under her shirt would talk and persuade even more convincingly the next morning.

The master made Vierra stand beside the table, where Ambjorn could see all of her in the glow of the fire. Ambjorn looked at her for a while.

"Unfortunately, I have to refuse your offer, but please do not be offended, for it is not for lack of your hospitality. The fault is mine. I do not want by my side a woman who only does it because she is told to."

A furrow appeared between the master's eyes. Normally, someone had to pay for that look with bruises and sores. The look disappeared as fast as it had come, however.

"So be it. I will fetch the beer." The master got up and left Vierra and Ambjorn alone together in the room in the longhouse.

Vierra looked at Ambjorn with fresh eyes. Viking men were stranger to her than the animals of the forest. The men of her own people could be fierce, but toward women they were always respectful, even if the woman was a bad hunter or from an unknown tribe. These men were different. They respected their own, but slaves were like cattle to them. Ambjorn's refusal had brought up memories in her mind, memories from a time when she had had some value, and her will some weight. Behind those brown eyes was hidden something that she hadn't faced during her three years of anguish.

"How do you live by yourselves, alone here in the middle of the forest?" Ambjorn asked Vierra, who was absently standing beside the table, lost in thought. The tone of his speech had changed from the stiff conversation of a guest, to a more direct, intimate one.

Vierra bent towards the man and whispered an answer. "Be careful, or you will stay, too. It's not easy to cross that forest. How on earth did you even manage to get here?"

Vierra's speech was cut off when Oder, who had noticed that the master had left, ran into the room. His hasty words flowed quickly, stumbling into each other.

"How did you cross the forest alive? Let us leave right now, this minute! Now is our chance. This is a sign from God, do you not understand this, man?" As he spoke, Oder grabbed Ambjorn by the shoulder, as if wanting to drag this large, seated man to the edge of the forest with his two hands.

Ambjorn gave Oder a resentful look and didn't move an inch. Emptied pints could be heard in his voice.

"Should I leave like a thief in the night and insult the hospitality that has been given to me? I do not think so. Your master has done nothing wrong, so I have no reason to be dishonorable." He swept Oder's hand away from his shoulder. Oder couldn't say a word, he just breathed heavily.

"Well, you are best judge of what you do," Vierra blurted. There was bitterness in her voice.

Ambjorn was about to answer when sound of the door opening interrupted him. The master had returned. He was carrying a small barrel made of dark wood. He ordered the slaves to the table and told Oder to get more wood for the crackling fire. Then he struck the barrel open and ran a thick, dark liquid into the guest's stein.

"This is my best and strongest beer. When I came to this place, that oak was already growing in the glade, just like it is now. I have always brewed a festive beer from its acorns and sap, one which I keep for special occasions. This is one of those."

The master filled his own tankard too, and drank a toast with the guest. Then he placed one more stein on the table and said, "Wolfgirl, now you will drink beer as well."

Vierra obeyed her master's order. The drink was bad and bitter, but it warmed her half-empty stomach fast. There was strength in the dark drink. Already, after one pint Vierra had to squint her eyes to see properly, and when she turned her head she felt like falling. The voices of the men mingled in her ears, and Vierra was no longer sure where they came from. There were other voices as well; strange, silent whispers that seemed to come through the walls.

The master's face glowed with satisfaction as he spoke over the table:

In the bowels of The Oak
Secret knowledge lies
Wisdom from the older time
There the sour lore cries

Hear me now you honored guest
See this woman clear
She is not a slave at all
Your wife is standing here

Ambjorn looked at Vierra, but his brown eyes did not see a thin, wiry slave girl. He grabbed the woman in his arms and carried her away with shaky steps, until finally laying her down on the wall bench, in the furthest corner of the house. The master's beer churned inside them both, doing its own magic. From the depths of the room came the master's laugh. Bitter and sardonic, it flew in their faces. It mocked their worthless wills, which the master seemed to hold in his grasp and direct according to every whim of his malevolent mind.

What happened between Vierra and Ambjorn wasn't at all unknown to her. Often, she had been forced into the act that men, through the ages, have been able to force women into. It had been violent and ugly, and a free woman from the Kainu tribe could not have imagined that kind of thing to even be possible.

This time, though, it was different. It was as if the man had opened a gate holding tenderness inside him and allowed the emotion to flow out. For many long years that gate had been closed, in the absence of any worthy recipient for that abundance of feeling and goodwill which this exceptional man carried within him. A man of his stature could not show that kind of weakness in the presence of other Vikings.

Deep in the darkness as Vierra was, the man still managed to find and touch her soul. Ambjorn blew to life that withering flame, which before had burned wildly inside the young woman, and set glowing a spark of hope amid all that cruelty and misery. The stream of passion took the woman with it and brought her back to life.

Vierra fell into a deep sleep, into a dream where she could hear a small voice from her stomach speaking.

"Can you see me?"

Vierra could. The girl had dark hair like she did and dark eyes like the master, but the man's evil had not infected her.

The girl caressed Vierra's hair with a solemn look in her dark eyes.

"I will wait for you until you are ready."

Vierra tried to answer, but her consciousness slid back towards the world of wakefulness, and the girl with her dark eyes faded away into nothingness.

Night still held dawn at bay when Vierra woke up in Ambjorn's embrace. The large man lay half on top of her, unconscious and breathing slowly. Vierra pushed him off her roughly, but he did not wake and simply slumped back to the bench. She dressed again in her woolen coat. There was warmth flickering inside her, even though her reason, languishing in darkness, gave it barely any value. She shook Ambjorn lightly but his state didn't change; the unnaturally slow breathing continued.

Vierra had never been in this part of the longhouse at this hour of the night. From spring till fall, the slaves had spent their nights in the summer hut, and the cold winter months locked into the end of the longhouse with the animals.

Vierra got up and looked around her. The glow of the fireplace had evened out to a reddish ember, which only brought a small amount of light to the dark room. The sinister shape of the master was just a black shadow, half lying on top of the table. Vierra quietly sneaked closer and noticed he was asleep. There were the leftovers of yesterday's feast on the table: a couple of chickens, skins of a ham and the bones of a large trout.

The knife she held behind her started to talk.

"Take me and strike deep. Now is your moment."

Yesterday morning, she would have obeyed the order, but the warmth that had been reignited in her heart woke up another voice, which rebelled against such a vile act.

The knife's voice was cold, metallic and strong, and the emerging warmth in her had no chance to subdue its will. Her hand moved shakily behind her back and coiled around the handle of the thick-bladed knife, one dirty finger at a time. How familiar the feel of that handle against her hand was. The knife rose up like a thought, ready to strike, and her green eyes stared at the hunched figure with an icy gaze. The master snorted in his sleep and Vierra instinctively jumped backward, knife still held up high.

"Not to gray ground, no. I will sleep with a sword and kill, kill them all." The man raved in his sleep with a weepy voice, and his hands alternately clenched into a fist, as if he were holding the hilt of a sword, and then flopped open. Vierra stopped to listen; she had never seen the master like this.

"I killed in the west and in the east. Everywhere. I will go to the halls of the heroes!" the master yelled, continuing his delirious dream.

Vierra's confusion disappeared and she stepped back to the table, intending to finish what she had started.

For such a large man, the master vaulted up with amazing speed. His half-dazed vision searched for something in the gloom, but then sharpened and saw Vierra beside him, knife held up high. A glimmer in his eye told of understanding, which led to a fast conclusion.

"Show me what you will, Oak, but this woman will not kill me."

The man leapt toward the woman and struck at her face with his fist. Normally, Vierra would have simply stood there and taken the blow, because it was pointless to run from an inevitable destiny. To his surprise, though, this time she ducked and dodged the incoming blow, thrusting her knife forward at the same time with both hands. The blade sunk a span's length into the master's chest. Vierra twisted the weapon to one side with all her strength, and with a crack it opened a gaping wound in the spot where the blade had struck. The slave woman had momentarily gotten back her fiery will. The fangs of the wolf were revealed again.

The Viking warrior who had lived through countless battles could not be slain with a single thrust, no matter how grievous. He punched with his left fist, aiming for Vierra's temple. The blow was so heavy that if it had met its target, it could surely have ended Vierra's life. However, she instinctively held up her shoulder and the blow landed there instead. Nevertheless, it sent her reeling all the way to the tamped earth floor of the house. Her shoulder burned and tingled. She shook her head, dazed, her eyes frantically searching for the master.

Her gaze found him standing immobile like a black colossus, the blade still protruding from his chest. Vierra crawled away, a primal panic washing over her. The master should be dead; anyone should be dead after that kind of stab. The red spot on the chest of the master's handsome linen suit grew, until it covered almost all of the front of the garment. The racket had finally wakened up Ambjorn, who got up clumsily and noisily, with no idea of what was happening.

The master did not see Ambjorn, he had eyes only for Vierra. For Vierra, and for the blade still sticking out of his chest. He yelled with a terrible voice.

"Why? Now I will go to the gray land of the shadows. Even though I waged war my whole life in strange lands, and I deserve to go the Halls of Heroes!" He let out a maniacal laughter. "Do you think you can leave? The Oak will not let you, the forest will not let you. We will meet in the gray halls."

Ambjorn stepped from the back of the room and finally got control of himself. The master fell to his knees as streams of blood trickled from his clothes and onto the floor. His fading eyes noticed Ambjorn.

"Strike me down, man, give me a sword and strike, so I won't go to the eternity of women and perjurers."

Ambjorn did not move. "I cannot. I have never killed a helpless man, nor a hospitable host. That would surely bring ill luck."

The master collapsedl onto his stomach and the knife sank up to the hilt in him and the red tip of the blade emerged through his back. Despite this, he was talking.

"Helpless, huh? I will kill all of you with my bare hands."

He started dragging himself forward on the floor with his arms, leaving a wide trail of blood behind. Even his warrior's strength had its limits, though. He trembled and his advance came to a halt. He exhaled once and went silent.

Vierra looked at her dead master, and the feeling of emptiness inside her did not change. Somewhere in the past she would have felt relief for the death of this tyrant, but now it had happened, she could feel nothing.

"We have to get out of here!" Ambjorn yelled and opened the door. He gasped the cool night air as if he had just stumbled out of a smoke-filled room.

The evening had turned into a grim night and, in the gloom of the house, the open door was like a window to the impenetrable darkness. A chilly night wind carried with it an invasive feeling. It was as if someone was watching them through the darkness, seeing them in the glow of the embers and feeling their movement on the hard, tamped floor of the house. Shivers ran through Vierra.

"Close the door fast," she said and wrapped her arms around herself. Ambjorn did not need telling twice. "The Oak and the forest won't let us go," Vierra continued ominously, peeking involuntarily at the body which lay on the floor.

"Let's feed the fire," Ambjorn said curtly. He dug large chunks of firewood from a box and threw them onto the embers of the fireplace.

"Do not put too much on or we will be smoked to death."

"I would rather die in light than in darkness. Where are the other slaves? We cannot leave them there, not now."

"In the summer hut, I think, but we cannot go out there."

Ambjorn took a large branch from the box and wrapped some dirty linen rags he had found hanging from the edge of the box around it.

"Is there any grease in here?" he asked.

Vierra fetched what the man asked for, and soon he had made a primitive torch out of the branch, linen and grease. He lit it up from the fire that rose from the fireplace. It burned smokily and unevenly, but it burned.

"Show me the way."

They stepped out of the door. Darkness attacked them and the little fire of the branch felt insignificant against its intrusive clutches. On the borders of their hearing were whispers which the night wind carried within it. Neither the cruelty of the master nor his atrocious act of rape had been able to touch Vierra's hardened mind lately, but those whispers made her neck hair stand up and brought cold twinges to the pit of her stomach. She instinctively moved closer to the man and his light-bringing torch.

They stepped to the door of the summer hut and opened the latch. Alf and Oder were awake.

"What has happened?" asked Oder.

"Your master is dead, let's go inside the house," replied Ambjorn.

"The Forest?" blurted Oder.

"The Forest," answered Vierra.

The Sacrifice

"Let's make torches for all of us and move in a line through the forest. God will show us the way," Oder suggested.

He, Ambjorn and Vierra sat as close as they could to the flaming fireplace. Alf was crouching by the master's body. It was impossible to tell from his face whether he was feeling joy, sorrow, fear or suffering. Maybe a bit of all.

Vierra looked at the silent man and a chill ran through her. That was the end of the road she was walking, too. In the end, slavery led you either to death, or to becoming like Alf, lost who-knows-where.

"You have seen for yourself what happens to those who escape," Vierra argued. "They do not get any further than a stone's-throw into the forest. And definitely not far enough not to be heard from here."

"*He* got here," Oder said and pointed to Ambjorn. "None of those that tried to escape had put their faith in God. Everyone just believed in the demons and devils of this land. And that forest is full of them."

Vierra was silent for a moment. For a long time, she had carried a bitter thought inside her. Her tribe members would shun it, that she knew for certain, but her fear couldn't fade it out completely. Now, for the first time, she dressed it up as words.

"I will not put my life in the hands of gods any more, be they those of the South or the North. We have to come up with something else. I'd rather even wait for the morning."

Oder looked sad. "Think about your child, if not yourself," he told Vierra. "I, for one, will go and I'll take Alf with me. Alf, make torches and pack some food into a bag."

Alf lifted up his gaze and started to follow orders. His hideous face twisted into a satisfied expression.

"Can you show us the way you came here?" Vierra asked Ambjorn.

"I do not know. We were bear-hunting when the sun suddenly blackened out and we were attacked by a group of indescribable... things, which I'd rather not remember." Ambjorn shook his head. "I took a blow to the head and I wandered half-conscious in the forest, and I have no recollection of how I got here. I woke up at the edge of your glade." Ambjorn sorted out the past events in his mind, his intense gaze on the crackling fire. Then his eyes strayed to Vierra and remained there, staring at her thoughtfully.

"It is madness to wait. I will go when the torches are ready. I will not stay here for one more moment," Oder spat out and hurried away to make his torches.

Vierra was filled with doubt. Entering the forest would mean death, and no god could protect them there. Her mind, which had woken up from numbness at last, was fighting to find an answer which could satisfy her moody, suspicious instinct. Her gaze circled the longhouse like a trapped animal. She stepped to the table, where a cask of beer stood, half full.

"You were not sane when you came through the forest. You were not sane when you drank the master's beer." Vierra looked at Ambjorn meaningfully. "Let us drink beer until dawn and leave at first light."

"By God's name, what madness!" Oder blurted. "Make torches and come with us. Surely, with the four of us, we can survive the forest with God's help." From somewhere about his person, he dug out the reed cross that he always carried with him.

Vierra grabbed the stein that lay on the table and filled it with the dark, bitter liquid.

"Do as you want," she said and poured the stein's contents down her throat.

Ambjorn hesitated as Alf and Oder prepared to leave. Silently, they gathered their gear and stepped to the door.

"This is your last chance," Oder warned Ambjorn.

He stood up, but Vierra gripped his hand tightly and said, "Believe me, if you want to live." Ambjorn stayed still.

Alf and Oder opened the door and disappeared into the darkness of the night, with no goodbyes from either side.

Ambjorn sat down at the table and took a tankard. He filled it to the brim and, keeping his eyes pinned to its foamy top, drank all of it down with one gulp.

"Do you remember what happened when you drank with the master?" Vierra asked.

Ambjorn did not answer immediately.

"No."

A second pint followed the first one, and a third one the second. Whereas before, Ambjorn had become more talkative because of the drink, now it turned both of the imbibers inward, and no more words were traded in the night that surrendered slowly to the morning.

Vierra's head was spinning and she got up to see if she could still stay on her feet.

"Shall we go?" asked Ambjorn. He gripped the edge of the table tightly as he got up.

"We shall," Vierra answered curtly. "Should we burn the house?" she added.

"Yes. Let it burn."

They took with them their steins and the cask, and stepped out of the door. The impenetrable night had given way on the eastern skyline, where daybreak was making its arrival. The forest waited for them, looming dark and threatening, and Vierra did not dare to look at the Oak.

They had spread the fire from the fireplace with wood, and soon, dried from decades of smoke, the old longhouse was ablaze. Like a hug yellow torch, it lit their way as they turned toward the dark forest. The strong drink churned inside Vierra, driving waves of confusion and nausea through her. Even despite that, she could not ignore the forest. Its challenge rose against them, gloomy and ancient.

Instinctively, a hand found another hand, body another body, as if seeking safety. Lifelong friends wouldn't have walked closer to each other than they did. Fear, greater than just the terror of death, drove them together. Vierra and Ambjorn looked at each other for a moment and, aiming toward the glimmer of the sun's first light, they stepped into the forest in unison, one step at a time.

The journey was a nightmare filled with confusion, where strange, tree-like shapes reached to grope them in the dark. Everywhere around them, the forest was whispering in its own secret language, scheming and plotting against them.

Often, a branch or a root tripped one of the travelers, and then the other dragged him or her back up immediately. In this way, they continued their desperate trek toward the dawn of the next day. They did not know if they were moving in a circle, but, whenever their confusion allowed, they tried to head towards the sun which was rising painfully slowly. The sounds of the forest grew from whispers to yells and from malevolence to hostility.

"Here you will stay, in the ground you will lay, join us you shall, the ranks of the gray."

A thick fog started to intertwine. It was so heavy, they couldn't see the rising sun anymore. The nearest trees just gleamed like foggy shadows amid a gray mass. They had lost their direction and, glancing around, they stopped and leaned against one another.

There were darker figures than the fog moving around them. Vierra blinked her eyes anxiously, thinking she was seeing visions created by her exhaustion, but the shapes didn't disappear. Instead, there were soon more and more of them, everywhere, surrounding them. When they came closer, Vierra and Ambjorn could see that they were shaped like men, like figures of people made out of fog. No artist could have depicted such lifelike creatures; they resembled real people, even down to the smallest detail. On every gray walker's eyes burned a white, milky shine which drilled into the travelers with an inhuman glow. There were women and children in addition to men and, to her horror, Vierra realized she knew a few of the shapes. Finally, they also saw Oder and Alf, and they didn't need to wonder about their destiny any more.

They felt as if the damp fog was strangling them. Vierra and Ambjorn fell to their knees, gasping for air greedily as if they had water in their lungs. Gulping the foggy air did not relieve the pain they felt inside.

In her mind's eye, Vierra saw glimpses of the miserable lives and deaths of these misty shades; the deaths that their master, Bothvar, had brought to them in his house. She also felt the anger that pulsated in them, hatred towards everything alive that didn't share their own fate. The visions invaded her mind like a dagger, deepening her anguish.

Oder's figure stepped forward.

"Here you will stay, in the ground you will lay, join us you shall, the ranks of the gray."

Oder's grey shade repeated this, and the others hummed it with him, one after another, until these words engulfed the whole fog-filled world.

Vierra's sight started to dim, and she couldn't make out the shapes clearly anymore. She could still hear herself talking and feel her mouth moving. But the voice that spoke wasn't her own voice, nor the will that moved it her own will.

"Spirits of the night, go away."

Vierra knew that voice and will. They belonged to the dark-eyed girl who had visited her dream.

The shadowy figures fell silent for a moment, as if listening, but then continued their humming with a hint of triumph. The fog grew thicker and thicker, and Vierra couldn't see the forest anymore.

"You know whose blood flows in me!" yelled the voice from inside Vierra again, full of staunch determination. "Blood is power. I have the might to command. Do you see? The fog is clearing."

Vierra felt that her hand made a gesture, moved the cloud of fog aside. It was her hand, but she wasn't controlling it.

The fog started to yield, and Vierra felt the squeeze in her lungs letting go.

Run, fools, run. I cannot hold them forever. Vierra heard a silent voice inside her head. She grabbed Ambjorn's hand and pointed at the sunrise which had appeared from the fading fog. He looked stunned, but let the hurrying woman drag him along with her.

They ran as fast as they could, considering their loss of breath and the fumes of the beer. The forest opened in front of them, seemingly endless, and disappeared behind. However, the fog didn't let go. It reached its gray fingers after them, over every tree root and to every hollow in the forest. Vierra felt the creatures behind her, even though she couldn't see them when she looked back. Ambjorn also seemed to understand; he moved fast, with sweat and dew dripping from his beard, and didn't look back.

Something strained its powers to their limit. From behind them in the forest, only low sigh could be heard, not much louder than a morning whoosh of wind. And as they walked, the fog couldn't reach them anymore and the sun rose over the treetops, painting the bleak morning sky blue as if to mark their final victory.

Vierra felt something break inside her. A sharp pain made her cower and forced her to lie down on the ground. Moss felt damp against her cheek.

"Sorry, Mother," Vierra heard a small voice inside her say. "It was either me or all of us."

"No, you can't! You can't!" yelled Vierra to herself. "I have nobody else."

In the already fading voice, there was sorrow:

"The Fargoer will not bear children. Once I have left you, you will never have a third. It is a dear price and a large sacrifice. Do not grieve, Mother, for we will meet on the other side by the fires of your foremothers."

Vierra felt something flowing out of her. She did not see dark hair or dark eyes, but Vierra knew that the child would have had those, had the girl been allowed to live. For a short moment, Vierra had felt something. Something other than three years of numbness caused by slavery. That something had now been ripped away from her.

Ambjorn half walked, half carried Vierra through the forest. He did not understand what had just happened, but didn't break the silence with questions.

Vierra and Ambjorn stood on the top of a hill, from where there was an unobstructed view to Ambjorn's home village. Two ravens soared high in the sky, and the clear autumn weather carried into their ears the voices of the people moving down in the valley. There was still a stench of burned wood in the air, even though the houses of the village had burned to the ground two nights ago.

Ambjorn's expression was grim as he looked down at the remains of his future. "We have to go down to help the others," he said and took a step down the slope.

Vierra stood there, not making a move. They had traveled in silence.

"Come on."

"Why?" Vierra's voice echoed with emptiness.

"I owe you for saving my life. You are alone, with no food or gear. You have no status, family or relatives. Someone will take you as their slave."

"I do not care."

Ambjorn's anger could be seen on his face. "*I* care. You'll be my slave from now on, then."

Ambjorn took her arm and pulled her with him, down the side of the hill. Vierra did not resist. At that moment, there was no purpose for anything.

Bloodsilver

Sea Sown Wishes

DRAGON-HEADED BOWS of two longboats appeared from the mist like ancient sea monsters. The sounds of men rowing the boats echoed strangely in the impervious air, mixing with splashes of water and oars creaking against damp, wooden surfaces. The late autumn weather in the Northern Gulf could change violently, offering a traveler anything from warm sunshine to a freezing blizzard. On the bows of the boats stood the lookouts, who stared constantly into the gray, damp wall that loomed out in front. They rowed in unfamiliar waters. Even the slightest error could mean a shipwreck on the icy sea.

The crew members, shivering in their rain-soaked clothes, knew exactly what kind of danger they were getting into. The men of the leading boat were long-bearded, proud Vikings. They traveled far during the summertime, wagering their lives and swords for bounty. Luck had not been on their side lately, thus encouraging them to journey this far, this late in the fall. The boat was led by Thorleik Styrsson, a heavily-built and cold-eyed Norseman. Numerous battles had left him full of deep scars, but had also brought him fame as an invincible Viking. It was the fruits of Thorleik's knowledge that they tried to reap now, and the thought of silver treasures burned in each and every mind like fire. The northern sea was an unusual target for plundering;

it would be hard to find anyone there boasting about the silver or gold they have. Nevertheless, the men believed in Thorleik; he had good luck and therefore his troops were trustful.

If the men in the first boat were tough as hardened oak, the crew of the second was carved out of softer wood. From their boat, the men watched the surrounding mist with nervous eyes, as if at any moment it could manifest itself in some threatening form and unleash its fury upon them. Most of them were unseasoned peasants, and only a few had seen enough seas and journeys to call themselves proper Vikings. They even had two women with them, something that disturbed the men greatly. Many of them were afraid of the water spirits' wrath and were often dropping crumbs of bread into the water to soothe them. The boat was led by red-bearded Ambjorn. Styr had been his father, too, and even though you could recognize them as brothers by their looks, their essence was altogether different. Ambjorn's face, unlike his brother's, was without scars; A fact that was not counted to his benefit in the minds of the men rowing his boat.

On the back of the boat, separated from the others as much as possible, sat two women. As odd as their presence on a journey like this was, their mutual differences were even more striking. The one sitting further away was tall and blond, an archetypal Svean woman. The blue eyes that glowed underneath the golden hair were like splinters of ice; eyes which she used to glare at the surrounding mist, as if detesting the trouble it caused to the travelers. It was useless to try and find any warmth in her stare, even when she was watching her red-bearded husband from the back of the boat. Her sisters did not traverse the sea nor travel and plunder, but took care of the cattle and homes while the men were away. Jofrid Olafsdaughter shared the destiny of her husband Ambjorn and of everyone on the boat; they had no home or cattle any more. Nevertheless, Jofrid was not a woman to bend in the face of hardship. Instead, misfortune gave her fierce strength to maintain the only thing she had left; her honor.

The other woman was dark-haired and much shorter than Jofrid. Her looks suggested northern origins and her frame a demanding life spent in nature. For the last few years, Vierra had been far from her foremothers' hunting grounds. Over three years ago, she had witnessed how cruel the men of these tall people could be. They had slain her husband and son, torn her away from her homeland and taken her far over the sea into a life of slavery. The time spent as the Vikings' slave had extinguished the sparkle from her dark eyes, and only tenacity and persistence had kept her alive. But now, every pull of the oars took her further away from a slave's life and closer to the land of her birth. Now and then, a glimpse of a rocky shore or outlines of a dark forest could be seen through the mist. At times, Vierra's eyes wandered to the crew of the other boat and when they found Thorleik, an open, uncovered hatred rose onto her face that did not go unnoticed by the target of the stare.

The autumn day cleared and the mist dissolved rapidly. The air stayed damp nevertheless, and gray clouds hung low above the dark sea. Free of the mist, the travelers could now see where they were going. The boats traveled along the shore northbound, and the thick forest that grew on the strand often reached all the way to the waterline. Autumn had already stripped the deciduous trees of their clothing, and they stretched toward the sea with their naked branches like skeletons. Here and there, the forest was breached by empty fields, already relieved of the crops, and occasionally the travelers could see glimpses of cattle and sheep. Other than that, the shores looked uninhabited. Now and then, on the hills that rose further away from the strand, there could be seen simple forts which often had signal fires burning on top of them. Fires had been lit because of the boats, but robbing farmers was not a part of their plan, and the boats kept moving towards the north instead.

When the day turned into evening, even the slightest signs of settlement disappeared, and their boats passed beside an untouched wilderness. Thorleik started scouring the shoreline, looking for a suitable camping spot. The wind had been weak all day, and the men had been forced to row the boats forward with no help from the sails. To add to their troubles, the clouds started to drizzle, which made the men shiver at their oars.

When the dusk set, they finally pulled ashore to a small bay. Styr's sons ordered their crews to collect firewood. Soon, there was more than enough, but everything was wet and the fire could not be lit, even with the best of skill. The tired, cold men cursed, when one attempt after another failed.

"Can't anyone get a fire going?" yelled Thorleik, annoyed by his men's misfortune. "I promise twenty silver coins from the bounty to the one who makes a fire now."

To everyone's surprise, Vierra got up and answered. "I can do it, if you let me go into the forest to find suitable wood."

Thorleik looked surprised. A promise was a promise, nevertheless, and given in front of the whole group.

"Pesky bondwoman, you are just trying to scheme your way to escape or to bewitch us. You are dark, and obviously a woodswoman. Is it not that this is your homeland, where you were born and raised?" he spoke, trying to renege on his promise.

"You should know where I grew up, for you have been there. Besides, I, like you, have a desire for dryness and warmth, and a woman's success should not bother a chief of your magnitude," said Vierra, with a hint of concealed ridicule in her voice.

Ambjorn suddenly intervened. "I will go and guard her, so she can't go anywhere. And she's my slave anyway, so if she does, then it's my loss."

Both Thorleik and Ambjorn's wife, Jofrid, looked at him askew. Why would a man protect his slave's business? However, as Ambjorn was the leader of the second boat, his word was obeyed immediately.

Vierra stepped into the dark forest with Ambjorn following closely behind. Thorleik had guessed wrong, as these were not her homelands. But, even if her native forests soughed much further to the north than this, the forest here talked in a language very familiar to her. It's damp, cool feel woke up memories and feelings, feelings which endless labor and cruelty during her years of slavery had extinguished. She breathed the forest deep inside her, and its strength straightened her stooped posture.

"What do you intend to do?" Ambjorn asked, as they walked further into the darkening forest. "You cannot lead me astray here."

"I'm just trying to get to warm myself, like I told you." In her voice was a little of the old willpower that she used to have.

After searching for a while, Vierra finally found a dry, resinous stump of a pine on higher ground, which was partly under the surface. No rainwater pooled here as it flowed easily down to lower ground. Vikings were able woodsmen, but they lived in houses and cultivated the earth. Vierra's people had lived in forests since ancient times and in their life, failure to make a fire equaled death. Ambjorn and Vierra went to work, and it wasn't long before their axes had broken off large pieces of the stump.

When they were already preparing to go back, Ambjorn suddenly grabbed Vierra by the waist and pulled her against himself. His hands were trembling from the surge of emotion he had been holding inside. Vierra did not return the gesture. Ambjorn pushed her away from him and she fell down onto a tussock.

"All of you are the same, cold as the winter's breath."

This kind of behavior was not unfamiliar to Vierra. Even though she had only been Ambjorn's slave for a short while, he had already done this countless times. And she had turned him down just as many times.

"Why don't you take what you want by force?" Vierra snapped. "That's what the other men of your tribe do."

Ambjorn looked surprised, because Vierra had never before responded to his approaches in any way. She had been like a dead fish in his large hands.

"I do not take love by force."

"You had maids and slaves. Why didn't you take them with you instead of me?"

Ambjorn thought for a moment.

"Nobody has the same kind of fire that you do. I know it burns inside you, even if you don't show it to anyone else. Why won't you give it to me? I have treated you well, better than anyone else. Do I not deserve your love? You have bewitched me."

Vierra tried to find signs of deceit in the man's eyes, or a glimpse that would tell something words never could. If Ambjorn remembered what had happened between them in the longhouse in the forest, he had kept it to himself. Something moved inside Vierra, something she had thought dead forever, but right there in the forest it started to slowly come back to life. Ambjorn was an exceptional man, and Vierra understood she could never find better in this cold and hostile world. She got up from the wet moss.

"Then come with me. Grab my hand and I will take you to the forest. Let's leave everything else and go back to my tribe's lands. There, I will share with you the joys and sorrows of my hut."

Ambjorn didn't answer for a long time. Finally, he admitted, "I cannot. I have my responsibility for my men. And for my wife's and brother's honor." He indicated for the woman to go back.

Vierra was surprised to find herself feeling disappointed.

Finally, the wood cutters returned to camp and Vierra started to light the fire carefully. A spark that she had struck was alive, and she fed it with small chips of the pine stump. For a moment, she paused, as if hesitating, but then she started to sing Birth of Fire in a clear voice, like she had done before when among her own tribe.

Oh you seagull, bird of birds
Strengthen here our pyre
Termes mighty, lord of heavens
Bring to us your fire

Give me now the brand of yellow
Spark of highest heat
Warmth to lonely forest dweller
Flame of life unsheathe

That was the first song that had come off her lips after her son had died. As if sensing this shackled power, the flames started to blaze and grow rapidly. The Vikings backed away from the singing woman, and looked at her nervously.

"The slave hag will witch us all. I think I will kill her," Thorleik stated.

"Let it go. Look, the fire burns warm and well," said Ambjorn, grasping his brother's hand and stopping it from reaching for a sword.

The rain ceased and the night fell, shrouding them and their small fires in darkness. Warmth, the cessation of rain, plus beer and food, heightened the group's spirits and soon the merry voices of chattering men echoed in the forest. They feared nothing, because the woods looked unsettled by any tribes, and two longboats full of men were a tough adversary to any war band that this land had to offer. After eating, the men went to sleep and only the ones left on guard stared at the crackling fire and talked quietly. The boat leaders were conferring about the upcoming day.

"Do we reach the treasure tomorrow?" asked Ambjorn.

"There's only half a day of rowing left," replied Thorleik. The glow of the fire made his scarred face look even more hideous. "Why does that wench slave of yours give me the evil eye? How much will it cost if I strike her dead? She brings me bad luck and women should not be present on this kind of journey at all," he said, with indignation in his voice.

Ambjorn considered his words for a moment.

"You know very well why the women are with us. And when it comes to Vierra, I hope that you won't carry out your threat. She was the one that made these fires, after all," defended Ambjorn.

"I remember your story. The story of a darkening sun, of combat and of a longhouse in the center of a cursed forest. And that woman rescued you from there... a woman!" Thorleik did not hide the mockery in his voice. Finally, he snorted: "It is useless to dwell on this. I will keep my sword sheathed for now. And you, brother, keep your slave in order and hope that your weakness does not drive us all to ruin, like it has driven you."

Ambjorn's eyes flashed with anger. A fight between them was not in question, however. They were leaders of their crews and on a joint quest. So they also lay down, tired from the day's burdens.

Ambjorn went to his wife's side on the hides, and she looked at her husband, her eyes bright in the lively gleam of the fire.

"Wouldn't it be best for all of us if we sank Vierra in the sea, or maybe left her here?" Jofrid asked her husband. "Men say women bring bad luck when searching for silver, so wouldn't it bring half the luck back if one of the two women was gone?"

"I will kill nobody for a paltry reason, especially someone who has saved my life," Ambjorn snapped. "It would bring twice the bad luck. Besides, if we find the treasure our father buried, we'll need good slaves to rebuild our village."

"Silver will buy slaves more obedient than Vierra," answered Jofrid.

Ambjorn didn't answer and they both fell silent and slept till the morning.

The Guardians

The morning dawned clear and cold. Wind had driven the clouds away and the sun rose, starting its daily passage through the blue sky. The men shivered and went about their morning errands briskly, to banish the numbness from their limbs. The boats were soon ready to go and everyone was eager to get their hands on the treasure. The rising sun and the rowing drove away the last of the cold from the men, and the air was filled with the happy hum of voices.

The rising sun was followed by a rather mellow wind from the southwest, given the time of the year, and the boats hauled their sails, which immediately bulged, promising fast and easy travel. The air warmed and the journey north progressed rapidly. The uninhabited shores were forested, but here and there were dunes speckled with pines and low, sandy beaches glowing golden in the sun. The terrain was flat, as if it had been cut straight with an enormous knife and, where the trees did not obstruct the view, they could see far inland.

"Are these regions familiar to you?" Ambjorn asked Vierra. He had walked to the aft of the boat, where the women sat in silence. Ambjorn evaded the woman's gaze and kept his eyes on the waves which gathered foam to the boat's stern.

"Our people sometimes come south, to catch salmon and otter. The hunters' luck has been always good, because nobody lives here. Old ones always warn about Termes' folk, the ones who guard these shores. They say people lived here once; people who came from the south and built houses and cleared land to grow their hay. The Termes' men drove them away and killed those who were not fast enough. They did not leave two stones side by side, or two logs together," Vierra said, remembering the stories the old hags had told her.

"This is where we will drive ashore, in any case. Thorleik said he had buried the treasure somewhere here with our father, a mile or more away from the shore."

"Then stay alert, or I will be left without a master again," Vierra whittled back. The closer she got to her homeland, the more the old Vierra came out, the one that had not been subdued by years of slavery. She looked into the man's eyes in a way totally unsuitable for a slave.

Sitting beside them, Jofrid listened to their conversation but could no longer contain herself. She slapped Vierra hard on the face with the palm of her hand and yelled, "You forget your place and rank, slave! We are not in your fathers' skin huts now. Do not forget it."

A fire, long thought extinguished, started to smolder in Vierra's eyes.

"Hit me again, go ahead. Your blows will not discourage me, unless you kill me. The time will come when I will hold an arrow on my bowstring and look into your eyes. Then we'll see how Olaf's daughter meets her maker."

"Ambjorn, are you going to let a slave talk to me like that and stain my honor? She has to be killed before she bewitches us all."

And Jofrid struck again, and a third time. As if all the anger pent up inside her was released, Jofrid continued to rain blows down on Vierra. The blows smarted, but Vierra didn't let it show on her face. She had been struck hundreds of times during her slavery. Those blows had been useless, because one who had been born amidst the backwoods spruce shadows, and no longer cared whether she lived or died, could not be subdued with fear or violence. Many scars they had left on her body, but her spirit had been hollow and heartless, impossible to influence. Now, after many years, the blows had gained an effect again, but it was not one Jofrid had hoped for. With every blow, the old, independent Vierra was growing inside the slavery-numbed woman, until finally Ambjorn grabbed her wife's arm, ending the punishment. It was at the last moment, as Vierra's bearing told that it would have soon turned into a battle.

"Enough! I shall not kill Vierra, as I owe her my life. If you want her dead, it will be up to a gathering's decision after we have returned. Either that or you will have to duel with her yourself. I will take no part in this matter before then. Slaves beaten half-dead are not useful, when the time comes to carry silver to the boat."

"You and your honor! How about mine, or ours? Maybe I will take other things to the gathering as well and return to my father's house." Jofrid huffed, rage in her gaze, but calmed down and sat sulking at the rear of the boat.

The men in the boat were silent. Their luck didn't seem to be about to take a turn for the better, no matter what. First, a strange group of men had burned down their village and now they were in this unknown land, on a journey led by Thorleik. None of them liked him, as he mocked them on every occasion, calling them earthdiggers and dwellers on the dry ground. Indeed, they also feared him, and for good reason. He had a fierce reputation and strong men with him.

Finally, Thorleik stopped the boats as they entered a bay and ordered them to be steered to the shore. The bay had a sandy beach, but the water was deep and looked like a boat haven shaped by nature. Midway along the beach were the remains of two longboats. The wooden boats had been mercilessly destroyed, even the sails had been torn to shreds. The men pulled their own boats to the shore and Ambjorn detached the dragon's head from the bow. Thorleik did not, and announced immediately that he was afraid of neither local nor foreign spirits.

After a few dozen yards, the sandy beach ended abruptly, as if it had been cut with a knife. That was the starting point of a plain, covered with rocks of different sizes. The rocky ground stretched inland for a third of a mile and followed the shore in both directions, at least for few miles.

"Here is where we fought for the silver, against a troop of men with sweaty coats," Thorleik mused. He shadowed his hideous face with his fist as he peered for the right direction in the bright sunlight.

"Do you know where these boats came from?" asked Ambjorn, as he looked thoughtfully at the two boats' remains.

"A silver-bearer's burden is often heavy. For many days we were followed by another ship, and we didn't dare enter combat with them at sea, given our heavy cargo. So, we decided to bury the treasure some way offshore and then confront them, on solid ground and without the burden. It was quite a fight, and only me, our father and few others managed to escape. We ran south, by land, until we managed to steal a boat from some fisherman. Father died on the boat, the enemies had wounded him too grievously. So, one of the boats is ours, but I do not know anything about the other one."

"So how do you know that the attackers have not taken the treasure?" Ambjorn asked, with doubt in his voice.

"I don't, but they didn't see where we hid it. Besides, do you have an option?" asked Thorleik, with a snort. Ambjorn did not reply.

They started their journey over the rocky plain. It was slow-going, because the rocks were slippery and covered with moss. Every man knew that, burdened with treasure, coming back this way would be much more difficult. Sun warmed the travelers and the autumn wind whistled through the forest that grew behind the stony soil. After crossing the rocks, the men stepped under the leafless birches and withered pines. The wind sang its hollow song in their ears.

Soon, they heard Thorleik, who was leading the group, cry out, "By Tor, look!"

And they all saw. Human bodies were hanging from the trees all around them. They were almost completely reduced to skeletons; whether it was because of the harsh northern weather or some dark force, nobody could tell. There they were, amidst the branches, waving grotesquely in the wind. Covering the weathered and wind-bared bones were torn clothes, of the type often favored by Vikings. Here and there on the ground were bones which had dropped from the bodies. Those who could still count, given their shock, saw over a dozen dead.

"Poor dogs! I wonder if it's our ambushers that are hanging there?" said Thorleik.

"This is the doing of Termes' Sons," said Vierra quietly, although not quietly enough not to be heard by others.

"We cannot stay here, either," said Thorleik finally, with forced calmness in his voice, and started to move forward.

"It is you who should be hung up here," hissed Vierra, this time so quietly that nobody else heard her.

Now, Thorleik's carefree attitude was gone, too. He organized the men to advance, so that a few scouts went ahead and a few others took care of the group's back. The grotesque forest changed into an ordinary one as Thorleik led them inland, towards a small hill a little more than a mile away. It was a good landmark on the otherwise level ground. The hilltop was covered with grass and rose just a bit above the tree-line. On the highest point was a circle made of boulders. The rocks were dark and partly covered with moss, and there was no roof, only rough, loose walls. The Vikings stepped towards it carefully. It had an aura of threat and unfamiliarity, which made anyone who approached it jumpy.

"We buried the silver in the center of that structure, and from there we will get it, too. Follow me," said Thorleik determinedly.

They stepped into the stone-circle, only to discover a maze-like stone construction inside. The rocks were twice a man's height, but misshapen, leaving the walls filled with holes from which the travelers could see into the inner parts of the structure. The entrance corridor continued along the outer edge of the building, but soon started to slope up, toward the inner parts. It formed a tightening spiral, which closed up to the center. The route was only a few men wide, and the Vikings formed a snake-like human chain as they walked into the circle's depths. In the middle of the building, the corridor opened up into a space where there was a large, flat and smooth stone. The shape of a sacrificial stone was familiar to everyone, but this one was bigger than they had ever seen. It was made of the same dark stone as the walls surrounding it, but it had been shaped into a bowl, stained brownish red and the outlines of a large hammer had been carved on its surface.

"The Termes' Hammer," said Vierra silently. "We are in the Giant's Guard, and it will be a miracle if we make it out alive."

"Witch, keep your mouth shut! That is Tor's hammer and it will bring us good luck," said Thorleik, with overconfidence in his voice. "I was here once before, and made it out alive then. Let us lift the stone. The silver lies beneath it. This stone was not here the last time."

Here and there on the floor was pieces of small, grayish-brown chaff. Ambjorn fiddled with it and grunted silently, "Bonemeal." Nobody said anything; only the wind hummed ominously in the cracks of the spiral.

The men got to work. They moved the heavy ritual stone and started to frantically dig the soil underneath. The ground was rocky and there was only enough room for a few diggers at a time. They dug in turns, letting a fresh pair of hands take over the work as soon as each digger tired. The sun had already started to set to the sea that waved gently in the west when, finally, the pickaxes and shovels of the sweating men struck an object that was rectangular in shape. They uncovered the lid of a great chest, made of wooden planks. When they ripped the lid open, they found a thick cloth in the chest below, which was torn off rapidly by greedy hands. Beneath the cloth were dust-covered piles of silver; jewelry, silverware, rings and buckles. Nobody in the group but Thorleik had ever seen such a treasure. The chest was so heavy that the men could not lift it up with its contents, and the artifacts had to be taken out one by one.

Thorleik stood in the chest and used both hands to stuff the valuables into sacks for the men to carry away. His beard was shaking and his hideous face twisted into a sunny grin.

"Didn't I tell you that our father's treasure was here, waiting for a taker? We will live in splendor for the rest of our days with these, every man of us."

The valuables were gathered into sacks, down to every spoon and buckle. The men were generous, and the treasure was divided into everyone's sack, roughly by weight. According to an old custom, the boat captains got five times the share of an oarsman and lookouts twice the share. With a long face, Thorleik gave Vierra a chalice weighing twenty silver coins, as the other men watched. This way, nobody could say that he wasn't true to his word. But he wasn't happy about doing this, and did nothing to cover his disapproval. Vierra received the prize eagerly, not because of silver but because of the discomfort it caused Thorleik.

Everyone, even Jofrid, soon had a sack to carry. They were eager to get away from the building and the group left, carrying the treasure without a specific order, hurrying towards the beach and the boats that waited there. Bad premonitions were with them, though, and they lengthened their steps under the load.

The group were just descending the side of the hill when, from behind them and close to the stone construct, they heard the sonorous sound of a horn. Its sound carried long and challengingly in the clear autumn air, until it died out, leaving only a ring of threat in the traveler's ears. The men halted at the sound of the horn, but Thorleik loudly ordered them to keep going. Nobody said anything, and they struggled greatly with their burdens. They arrived back to the forest of the hanging dead, and the men started to think that the horn might have been just a product of their tired minds. The forest was as silent as it was when they had first arrived, and there was no sign of an enemy.

Finally, they reached the field of rocks, and it was then that they heard sounds of pursuit coming from the forest behind them. Ambjorn and Thorleik herded their men into the rocks, behind which loomed the beach and their boats as a haven of safety. The men stumbled and cursed, exerting themselves to the limit. They were already getting closer to the seaside edge of the rocky plain. There and then, the forest revealed their pursuers to them as they rushed out of the woods.

If the Viking men were tall, even the tallest were a head's length shorter than these creatures. Their features were long, as if stretched by some unknown hand and from their beardless faces beamed a primal bloodlust. The skinny upper bodies of the monsters were naked, and their chests and sides were decorated with blue, saw-edged lightning zigzags and spiral drawings, which resembled the stone structure on the hill. In their hands they had clubs and axes made of stone which they brandished towards the Vikings, letting out a bestial battle cry. Then the creatures started to cross the rocks, leaping from one to another on their long legs with inhuman speed.

"We cannot make it to the boats before they'll be on us," Thorleik screamed to the struggling men.

"Let us group to the edge of the sand. We can just make it there," replied Ambjorn, already commanding the first of his men who had made it to the beach to ready themselves for combat.

The men grouped themselves at the edge of the stones, so the enemy could not reach even ground. Vierra dropped her sack of silver onto the sand, and, wiping sweat from her eyes, called to Ambjorn, "Give me a bow!"

"You think you can use it better than my men?" Ambjorn asked, with doubt in his voice.

"Believe me," Vierra said and looked Ambjorn in the eyes. Her wish was granted and the weapon, one of the few they had, was placed in the woman's hands, together with a quiver full of arrows.

The bow felt like an old friend in Vierra's hand, one she had been separated from for a long time. Her green eyes turned to the beasts that were running over the stony field, and none of the arrows she set loose missed its goal.

The creatures, however, did not easily fall to the arrows. Two, three, sometimes even four deadly-aimed arrows were needed to take down one attacker. The archers did not have time to fell many enemies before they had crossed the stone clearing and were on the Vikings.

A fierce battle for life and death began on the beach. The Vikings had good weapons and a better position on the even sand. The creatures of the forest, on the other hand, were bigger, and there was primal strength in their thin, sinewy limbs. Three times the attackers pushed the defenders backwards, and three times the creatures were pushed back to the rocks. Thorleik fought among the boulders, against multiple enemies, a thick froth gushing from his mouth. Ambjorn, who had lost his helmet, managed, with the help of a few of his men, to push the last of the monsters that had reached the sand back into the rocks.

Finally, a handful of the creatures, the few still alive, escaped over the stone field toward the darkening forest, the defenders' hoarse cry of victory following them. But one creature had slipped to their rear and now approached the boats.

"Stop it quickly, before it destroys the boats!" shouted Thorleik. And truly, the creature was holding an enormous boulder which it had dug from the waterline. It hefted the stone high above its head with both hands. Vierra shot an arrow that pierced the beast's heart, but, as the creature went down, it used its immense strength to hurl the boulder, which crashed into the middle of Ambjorn's boat, throwing splinters and seawater all around.

Honor and Death

The battle was finally over, but the Vikings had paid a dear price for their victory. Half the men lay on the sand, torn apart or struck dead, and many of the survivors had wounds and bruises all over their bodies. Ambjorn's group had suffered the most casualties, because they knew little of the ways of the battle and were badly equipped. There was a gaping hole in Ambjorn's boat, but so was the case with Ambjorn himself. He was lying on the sand, gasping for breath like a fish on dry land. A trickle of crimson blood flowed from the side of his mouth, tangling with his red, messy beard. Jofrid sat at her husband's side, trying to mend his broken body in vain. The sculpted pride and harshness had vanished from her bearing, washed away by genuine fear and worry, which was something that had not shown on her face for a long time.

As Vierra approached her former master, Jofrid lifted her eyes and hissed, "Get away, slave. Is nothing holy to you?"

With a tremendous effort, Ambjorn lifted his head from the ground as blood gushed out of him with increasing speed.

"Be quiet, you cold woman!" he thundered. He turned his eyes to Vierra. "Maybe I should have left with you."

Vierra said nothing. She just helplessly watched her master's struggle for life.

"Burn me and my dead men in our boat ... Promise me, woman, that you won't leave me here to be ripped apart by the creatures of the forest. That, if anything, you owe me."

Jofrid nodded, saying nothing.

"Ask my brother to come here. I want him to hear my last will."

"Very well."

Thorleik came over, soaked in the blood of the enemy, with a dripping sword in his hand. Vierra moved aside, as if controlled by her grim instinct.

"How is it?" he asked.

"I have fought my final battle. Lousy was my luck in arms. Father did right when he ordered me to take care of our homestead, and took you with him to the sea. But my luck wasn't good back home, either. So ends the story of the Son of Styr. Promise me, brother, that you will bring my wife back home."

Thorleik was no man to talk to the dying, and he didn't even try to embellish his answer. "That I'll do, if there's anything left for her there."

"With the silver, you can rebuild what has been destroyed."

Ambjorn's feverish gaze circled around until it found its target. Vierra was walking a short distance away on the beach, gathering arrows.

"I wish to release Vierra from slavery. Let her ashore at any harbor she wants, and give her five pieces of silver from my share. With those, she can continue her life as she wishes."

Thorleik's expression was gloomy.

"This wish I do not want to fulfill. Your bondwoman is to blame for our misfortune. My men heard how she had foreseen our destiny, and it is my intention to slay her. Death will release her from slavery, so your wish shall thus be partially granted."

With a painful effort, Ambjorn rose to a half-sitting position. His brown eyes burned with anger.

"Should you do that, I will curse you and your ship ten times with the bad luck of a dying man! Never have I killed anyone without a good reason, and my death will not be used as a reason for such a deed." A thick gush of blood burst from his mouth, and he fell back on the ground on his back, twitching.

Thorleik was angered and he shouted loudly, as if trying to reach his already unconscious brother.

"For cursing me, I will not fulfill any of your requests! I shall sell your wife as a slave for the eastern traders, and sell your men to row the most miserable boats of the fat Christian priests to their stinking cities!"

And so died Ambjorn, son of Styr. But Vierra, who had been standing unnoticed near her dying master, had heard everything that was said. And then, the old Vierra took a grip of her and wrested off all bonds of the dark years of the past. Her green eyes burned again, just like they had done long ago.

Now, she stood with her bow drawn and an arrow on the string, ten paces from Thorleik. She raised her voice and, in the clear evening, it carried to the ears of the men who were still recuperating from the battle.

"Ambjorn's men, hear me! Your master has fallen and, like you all heard, Thorleik is going to sell you for rower slaves and get fat with your shares of the treasure in some warm harbor. But there are many of you still alive. Are you just going to submit and bow your heads to Thorleik? Will you disgrace your master's memory by bowing to the will of another power, and give away your future to the hands of this hideous man? I doubt that you are men at all, if you let yourselves be led like sheep."

"Fool of a wench! We will trample you and all your allies into the sand. That will leave more silver for each of us!" yelled Thorleik, enraged, and he approached Vierra with his sword unsheathed.

Vierra skillfully shot an arrow which flew between his legs, making him stop his advance. She pulled another to the string, faster than anyone could see in the dusk.

"You will not butcher me like a lamb, Thorleik, even though you did that to my husband and son years ago. Your scabby face was branded on my mind forever when you came and destroyed my life. But even then, you didn't get me without a fight." Vierra's long, dark hair fluttered in the evening wind, and it was as if she looked taller than her normal short stature.

Thorleik's eyes narrowed with anger. "I wondered where I had seen you before. Your whole tribe should be wiped out. Your weak men let women control them and do naught but sit in their leather huts."

"Yes, so they do, and those Vikings who wander too far in our land, we put onto stakes for seagulls to peck, and to warn others. And you, Thorleik, I will shoot you if you come a step closer, and I assure you the next arrow won't miss."

An uneasy silence descended on the shore. Thorleik's men dared not stop Vierra for fear that she would shoot. But after a while, Ambjorn's men stepped behind Vierra, one after another.

"So, Thorleik," challenged Vierra, "shall we do battle right here and now, for the ownership of all the silver? It looks like, if we can send even a few of your men to the land of the shadows, you will not have enough rowers left to control your boat with the silver cargo. And the killing will start with you. On the other hand, if you don't want to fight, you can take your men and your share of the silver, and sail where you like with your boat intact. Decide quickly, for the evening is running out and my hand is getting restless on the bowstring."

Thorleik thought for a long time, his eyes flashing.

"A thousand curses on all the power-hungry women on this earth! I promise, before you and all the men, that I will come and find you and send you after your son and husband, to a place you won't come back from."

"I hope you will come, for on another occasion my hand will not hold back the arrow."

Jofrid sat on the beach beside her husband's body, stunned by the twists and turns of the events. Thorleik's men started to collect their treasure and belongings, eying Vierra and Ambjorn's men suspiciously. They left the dead where they lay, and it wasn't long before their boat moved away from the beach, towards the red sun that was setting to the sea.

Vierra started to act as if driven by an inner rage. A few able men were left to fix their broken boat with the parts of the two old boats that were rotting nearby. The remaining pieces of boat were pulled further away on the sand, and the men who had died in combat were piled up on them with all their gear. Ambjorn was placed on top. A sword and a broken shield were placed beside him, and, on top, pieces of equipment taken from the foes he had vanquished. They started the pyre from many spots. Against all odds, it caught alight, and the damp, rotten wood burst into flames. The hungry fire rose high in the darkening sky, and the men collected all their gear and treasure and loaded it into their boat, readying it for their departure. Some wondered whether the pyre would entice the Sons of Termes to attack them again. Nevertheless, they wanted to stand beside the flames and thus escort their master on his journey to the other side.

All this time, Jofrid had remained sitting on the sand, not once lifting her eyes. As the men followed the pyre, Vierra drew her bow and yelled.

"Hoa! Jofrid, my prediction came true. I have a bow, and you must make your choice here and now. Either you get on the boat, or try your luck here with the Sons of Termes."

For the first time since Ambjorn's death, Jofrid lifted her head and looked at her former slave with cold, empty eyes. "Like you said, we'll see how I face death. I will face it differently than you mangy dogs of leather huts would. I will face it like our foremothers have through the ages."

Jofrid rose slowly and walked straight into the flaming funeral pyre. Not one grimace of agony showed on her frozen face as the flames swallowed her. And so Jofrid followed her husband, and a gust of wind spread the ashes rising from their fire onto the sand and into the darkening sea. When the men finally turned their faces away from the pyre, Vierra was nowhere to be seen. It was as if the evening wind had taken her with it, leaving no trace behind. The men looked at each other for a moment, and then quietly hurried to the boat.

From far away, Vierra looked at the last red glow of the pyre. There, on the side of the forest that darkened to night, she finally let everything out. For the last three years she had been dead inside and without any feeling, and nothing could have hurt her. Now, she felt that the surge from inside her was taking her with it. Powerless, she fell to the moss, unable to rise.

With her tears came the sorrow and weakness that she had carried inside for so long. She cried for her husband Vaaja and her son Vaalo. She cried for the dark-haired girl that she had never had the chance to embrace and for those wise, dark and unborn eyes that waited for her on the other side. She cried for her own miserable destiny and her torn life. She also cried for Ambjorn, the only man who had cared for her in this repulsive world, and had never had his love returned. She cursed and cried for the First Mother. She cried for a long time, and was alone.

The pyre had also consumed her old life, the one maimed by slavery. Vierra turned her wet eyes towards the forest that loomed darkly in front of her. There, a future, filled with independence and insecurity awaited her. The she-wolf talked to her again. It was like a beast that had been chained up and was finally unleashed. Wild and savage was the spirit of the wolf, and it forced her to get up; to wipe the tears away from her green eyes; to step forward to the shadow of the trees that were growing ever darker.

The Song of Wolf and Moose

Tracks on the Snow

LARGE, SILVER-MANED wolf sat in the shade of the forest, waiting. The wait was shortly rewarded; moments later, a female moose ran heavily through the wintry wilderness that was gilded by the bright sun. The graceful legs of the animal sank deep into the snow with every step. Running in those conditions told of immense strength and endurance. The wolf smelled the moose's strong scent, the strength and fear of a fleeing animal.

The wolf waited patiently and let the moose pass by, which was something its kin would hardly have done. A moment later, three human pursuers appeared. The morning snow carried them on their skis, nicely speeding up the chase. The men were young, almost boys still. From underneath their caps flashed hair as yellow as the autumn hay. The patched clothes they wore had seen better days. The last of them was pulling a sledge made out of wood and covered with worn skins. Two of the men were short of stature, which was common to northern folk, but the third was sturdier and almost a head above them. As they passed, the smells of smoke, hunger and despair wafted to the keen nostrils of the wolf.

As it watched the men drawing away, a black-haired woman skied past its lookout. As far as her physique was concerned, she could have been related to the men. Her short figure was draped in deerskins and furs, and on her back a bow swung to the rhythm of her skiing. For a while, the wolf watched the receding shape of the woman and then silently slipped back into the shadows of the forest.

She moved with a familiar, even pace, which swallowed miles but did not fatigue her. Vierra was preoccupied, pondering over what to do. She had been following the moose tracks for over a day now when, by chance, a party of hunters had started to pursue the same animal. Now, they had caught the trail ahead of her. She had escaped the clutches of her Viking slavers last autumn but something prevented her from going back to her own people in the north.

After the Vikings had killed her husband and son, her closest relative was Aure, her cousin and a chieftain of the tribe. There was bad blood between her and Aure which went back far into the past, all the way to the spring of their adulthood when she had made a choice. A choice between death and life. It had driven Vierra to live the life of a loner and it had led her to where she was now. What mattered then, and still mattered now, was that it was her decision.

So Vierra lived a wandering life, alone in the wilderness, which was, especially during the winter, something that only the best woodsmen could survive. This year, the merciless north wind had blown colder than usual, as if wanting to destroy the lonely woman. Hunger was a familiar companion and it had eaten away at the sturdy layer of flesh and muscle she had developed in Ambjorn's slavery, leaving her thin and diminished. Even now, hunger was gnawing in her guts and whispering in her ear, tempting her to reckless acts.

Vierra disregarded their demands and settled for following the men from a distance, skiing in the weak trail they had left behind. The weather was perfect for hunting moose as the snow had a tough crust that could carry the skier all morning, whereas the moose's thin legs sank deep into the snow, which tore and tired them with every step.

The morning passed and the young men skied, keeping their prey constantly on the move. From the west, the wind drove thick clouds to the sky and the crisp frost soon turned to a thaw. The snow's surface ceased to carry the skiers and large, wet snowflakes started to float slowly down from the sky. As Vierra rapidly gained on the men, she noticed that here and there, the moose's trail was speckled with droplets of blood.

When the escaping moose finally ran into a thick forest, she managed to ski closer. The men stumbled as they followed the trail into the thicket and Vierra saw that they were exhausted. The men had skied too fast the whole morning, possibly assuming that they'd catch the moose sooner. In the sinking snow, the sledge started to weigh heavy and slow them down. Then and there, persuaded by her hunger, Vierra decided to act.

Her plan was to go round the trio that blundered among the branches, and also the moose that ran for freedom. She tried to get in front of the animal and into a good spot for shooting. Hunting knowledge, inherited from her foremothers, told her to go round from the east, but her own instinct drove her west. She rarely opposed her inner feelings, but now she hesitated for a moment, unable to reach a decision. The wind, blowing from the west, would carry her scent straight to the moose that was struggling in the thicket and could scare the animal, causing it to change its direction, which would have been disastrous for Vierra.

The she-wolf inside got the best of her, and Vierra finally decided to follow her instincts. After going around the thicket from the west for a while, she noticed that the wind had started to act up and blow from the east for a moment. Choosing the other direction would have been her undoing, as the moose would surely have picked up her scent with its sensitive nostrils. Thankful, she skied forward as fast as she could, being weakened by hunger, and her hopefulness rose with every swish of her skis.

After skiing for a while, Vierra stopped to rest in the thicket, sweaty and shaking, clinging to her luck. Following the sweat came shivers of cold and the nausea that followed the act of having exerted herself whilst suffering severe hunger. She managed to calm her empty stomach, though; vomiting and shooting a bow at the same time was not possible and she would only have one chance, if that.

A moment passed and the female moose charged from the forest toward Vierra's hiding place, the frozen terror of desperate flight in its eyes. Two feathered arrows stuck out from its sides. The men had reached shooting distance, but their bows had not been able to deliver death accurately enough. Letting the animal come as close as she dared, Vierra stood up and released an arrow in one movement. The sharp arrowhead sank into the base of the moose's neck, from straight in front of the animal. The moose grunted and halted in its tracks as if hit by a solid rock. It attempted a feeble escape toward the thickets as blood spurted from the grievous wound onto the snow.

Vierra skied fast after the moose and found it lying in the thickets a dozen paces away. It twitched a few times and then surrendered its life, as blood gushed intermittently from the gaping wound in its neck. The veneer of civilization was left at the feet of screaming hunger and Vierra stormed towards the moose, to drink greedily of the warm liquid of life that was spurting out. In the past, she would have poured blood onto the ground as well, giving her thanks to Mother Earth or the Seita. She had, however, started to shun ceremonies more and more, as she did now.

Suddenly, the men skied into view. They stopped, astonished, seeing the prey they had followed for so long already felled, and an unknown woman by its side. Vierra wiped blood from the sides of her mouth and yanked an arrow on the string of her bow. The young men also groped at their bows and one of them yelled, "Hoa! What wisp are you that slurps blood here? You may have gotten the moose, but the quarry is ours, for we have been chasing it all day."

"I am human just as you are, and not a malicious fairy. And you can hunt an animal for as long as you like, and still it won't be your catch unless you are the one who fells it."

"There are three of us, but you are alone. Surely you would not dare to defend the bounty against us?"

"You look like Kainu, but maybe you have lived this far south for too long. If you still respected the ways of our people, you would know that the feller of the prey has the right to decide its destiny. I am of chieftain's blood. I am a woman. Perhaps you have forgotten the teachings of the old crones since you came this far to the south."

"We haven't forgotten them. We just haven't had a sight of a woman since last summer. And our hunger is grave – so grave that we may well throw the old traditions out for the wolves."

"I am as hungry as you are. I would rather die here quickly, fighting you, than die slowly lying in the snow. I wouldn't want to kill men of my people, though, and a moose feeds more than one. I see that you have a sledge. Does that mean that you also have a village, or a winter camp? I suggest that we make a fire and sate our hunger together, and then ski to your village where we can share the meat with your kin. All I want, and may I remind you my demand is perfectly reasonable as the kill is mine, is a week's share off the carcass."

The young men looked doubtful for a while. Hunger was on her side, however, and they finally accepted her proposal. It didn't take long for the handy woodsmen to gut the moose. They obeyed the traditions and drained its heart's blood to the ground saying thanks to Mother Earth as the old custom demanded. Meanwhile, Vierra set up a crackling fire, in which they started to roast the fresh meat on the ends of wooden sticks. The meat was tough, and scorched on the surface while still being raw inside. Even so, Vierra couldn't remember eating anything half as good and gobbled down the meat, large chunks at a time. From the way they, too, were stuffing their mouths with the barely cooked flesh, the men's thoughts were the same. The sounds of smacking lips mingled with the crackling of the wet branches in the campfire, until their stomachs were full.

Only after they had eaten did the men introduce themselves as Ulva, Raito and Armas. Ulva was the oldest of the group, if one could call a boy of eighteen summers old. He was loud, had a hooked nose and seemed to be the undeclared leader of the group. Raito did not speak after the introduction, but sat, tall and serious, while the two shorter men did the talking. Armas was the youngest, a bit insecure, but an observant and talkative young man nevertheless.

"It seems you've followed the moose since the morning," said Vierra finally, smoothing her tightly combed hair back with the moose fat that was left on her hands.

"Yes, and the journey home will be arduous. We must go soon if we are to make it back before dark. Otherwise it might be the wolves that feast on the meat and not us. There are a lot of them around in these parts," said Ulva, in a serious tone.

"Let's do it then," answered Vierra bluntly and stood up. She covered her head with a fur cap and put on her skis.

They lifted the moose carcass onto the sledge and started to haul it toward the men's home village. The journey proved to be trying, however. Even though the sledge slid well, there was a lot of weight on it now and the snow didn't carry it well anymore. They set two skiers to pull the sledge while the other two went forward and opened up a path for them. They took only one short break but the night still started to darken frighteningly fast.

"I think a pack of wolves is following us," said Armas, ever aware of his surroundings.

"We will soon have to stop for the night or we won't be able to see well enough to make a fire," yelled Vierra to the two men who were clearing the track.

Nobody resisted, as it was still a long way to the village. They stumbled from fatigue as they started to gather branches and stamp the snow for a campsite. The campfire had to be lit quickly if they wanted to make sure the wolves weren't encouraged to attack in the dusk. Vierra got on with the task immediately while the others gathered more firewood. She struck the fire skillfully and the wood started to burn with a small, flickering flame.

"We need more firewood and bigger pieces. If the fire dies, so do we. Raito and Armas, come and tend to the fire while I go and find a log with Ulva," yelled Vierra, over the sputtering flames. Her face was smudged with soot and her clothes wet from crouching in the snow.

Ulva skied on ahead of Vierra, further into the dark forest, in order to find suitable firewood. As soon as he disappeared into the dense thicket there were sounds of a scuffle and Vierra hurried closer. She fired an arrow into the middle of the bushes and a wolf escaped with a yelp of pain. Ulva came out of the brushwood, groaning and holding his leg.

"What a shot in this darkness!" said Ulva to Vierra who approached with her skis.

"Are you badly hurt?"

"I'm fine," he replied. "Let's go and fell that tree."

The wolf had attacked him on the edge of the bushes but Vierra's arrow had driven the beast and its companions away, at least for now. They skied fast to a large sapling and Ulva chopped it down with his axe while Vierra kept guard, in case more wolves should appear.

Together, they pulled the felled sapling to the fire as the darkness closed them into a small islet of fluttering light. The sky was still thickly clouded, making the night's darkness totally impenetrable.

"Let's keep the fire high and the wolves away," Ulva stated, while rolling his ragged pant leg up from the wolf bite. The wound was worse than he had admitted. The beast's teeth had pierced the skin and dug deep, all the way to the bone. The punctures bled considerably but he was not in any immediate danger.

"I have no medicine with me and I don't think you do you, either. We'll just have to sew it and hope for the best." Vierra brought out a thin bone pin. Then she stitched the wound with a thread made of dried animal tendons while Ulva grimaced, clenching his teeth in pain. He didn't complain, though, as that would have made him seem weak in front of this outsider woman.

The hunters now made themselves as comfortable as they could by their wintry campfire. Skins were detached from the sledge and spread out by the fire and used as mattresses and blankets for the group that slept close together. One was put on guard, to care for the fire and keep an eye out for wolves. Now and then, a sad howl could be heard from the surrounding darkness. The beasts hadn't given up yet. Everyone was tired from the day's exertions and, after a quick dinner of some more venison, the men went to sleep.

Vierra took the first watch and sat by the fire, singing quietly to herself. She constantly peered into the surrounding darkness, but no wild beasts came to try their defenses. She looked at the sleeping hunters who were illuminated by the flames. Ulva turned from side to side, as if chasing the moose even in his asleep. Raito slept quietly and still, very much the same way he always was. Vierra's attention went to Armas, who was also sleeping peacefully. This lively young man stirred up memories of her own son. The same kind of blond hair and freely flowing mind connected him with her son, who had died years ago. Vierra sighed and released her gaze from the sleeping boy and the faraway memories in her mind.

When her watch came to the end, Vierra woke up Raito to take his turn as guard and then tried to get some sleep on the furs. For a moment, her natural suspicion prevented her from falling asleep. Eventually, reason and fatigue won, for she couldn't sense any deceit or threat in the men's behavior. In the forest, you had to get used to trusting even complete strangers, because sometimes, it was the only way to stay alive. Vierra lapsed into an uneasy sleep as Raito added more wood to the sputtering fire.

She snapped awake to gentle shakes from Ulva. Even though springtime was on its way, the nights were still long. The dark hours after midnight were upon them and the firewood was about to run out. In order to save the little they had left, they let the campfire burn down to embers and kept their eyes focused on the dark forest. There was movement to be seen now and then, on the edge of the fading circle of light, and you could hear the sounds of paws over the crackling of the fire. The wolves were still out there and the diminishing flames tempted them closer and closer.

"There goes the last of the firewood," said Armas. There was fear in his voice and in his eyes that gleamed by the glowing fire. The fire brightened for a moment, throwing sparks high up into the air.

"You keep your arrows and your knife ready. We haven't been eaten yet," Vierra stated encouragingly and stepped nearer to the boy. "Stay close to me." The young boy's fear awakened her maternal instinct. She stood by the fire that slowly waned into embers, with an arrow poised on her bowstring and her green eyes flashing. Frighteningly fast, the campfire dimmed to a faint glow while a pale hint of light could be seen on the eastern horizon.

When the morning glimmer created a grim, dark-blue moment, the wolves began their attack. They came simultaneously and from multiple directions, as if the surrounding forest was shooting dark gray arrows over the deep blue field of snow. Vierra's bow sang the vivid song of death and many of the dark gray arrows halted midflight on the snow, stopped by a smaller and even angrier arrow. The men were busy with their bows, too and it wasn't long before the remaining wolves gave up and fled back to the shelter of the forest.

"Let's pack our gear and leave. They'll linger nearby, anyway, waiting for another chance," said Ulva. He plucked the arrows off the bodies of the fallen wolves.

"Let's gather these first," Armas said and started to skin one of the animals. "These pelts are valuable."

"Take the flesh, too. If everyone else in your village is as hungry as you, it'll come in handy," Vierra ventured.

"Runtamoinen will not like it, and he probably won't like the skins, either," Armas mused.

"Don't care about Runtamoinen," the taciturn Raito snorted. "We'll just say that it came off a moose, and he will happily eat it."

"It's not wise to annoy Runtamoinen. He is more powerful than all the other villagers combined," said Ulva, in an irritated voice.

"That is his apprentice talking. His powers have not gotten your stolen women back, or taught us how to preserve game," answered Raito.

An uneasy silence fell over them as they prepared to leave. Raito and Armas skinned the wolves as fast as they could, and Vierra loosened the largest pieces of meat, to be taken with them. There was no time for accurate work, so the flesh was randomly cut. Ulva did not participate, but focused on gathering their gear and readying them for departure.

"A Songman's minion," whispered Ulva, staring at tall Raito. He spoke softly, so nobody else could hear him.

There was almost a sad look in the yellow eyes of the silver-maned wolf as it observed its brothers that had fallen to the snow. It didn't join the escaping pack, though, but watched the hunters from the safety of the darkness, alone.

Men of the Two Houses

The blue moment quickly changed to a dawning day. The wind had turned to the north and drove the clouds into shreds all over the sky. The freeze tightened its grip and the wind now blew cold. The yellow eye of the sun that now and then peeked from between the clouds was cold, too and couldn't give any warmth to the travelers. The snow carried a bit better now, though, and the wayfarers, strengthened by the meat they had eaten, moved briskly onwards on their skis. Even Ulva, with his wounded leg, skied surprisingly fast. When Vierra asked how he was doing, he only said he felt great. They arrived at the village a little before midday.

The village had been built on top of a low hill, to the side of which ran a small brook. The stream was now covered with ice and, in the pale light of the early morning, the village looked as if it were slumbering under the ice as well. The southern people wouldn't even have called it a village, so primitive and small were the buildings. Unlike the long log houses of the south, these were timber lean-tos which had been built against each other and had had crude fireplaces added to the ends. There were three of these lean-tos and one of them had been used to house domestic animals. The animals had been slaughtered a long time ago in order to quell the villagers's ever growing hunger. A few huts, made of long wooden poles and covered with moss and skins, decorated the view as a reminder of a phase, just passed, when their lifestyle demanded moving around after prey.

Normally, any arrivals would have been surrounded by a bunch of curious children, but in this village the yard stayed empty. After a moment, fewer than a dozen men emerged from the so-called houses to look at and ponder about the travelers that had arrived. They were like scrawny, starving dogs that had received too many beatings. Their grim expressions changed to joyous ones, though, when they saw the meat in the sledge.

The men dashed to the moose carcass like rabid animals and started to rip pieces off it with the tips of their knives. They shoved these into their mouths raw, to soothe the burning need inside.

"Get the sweat hut ready for the hunters, and make fires. Today we will feast." The speaker was a tall, middle-aged man, who stood out from the others by dint of his stick-straight posture and burning blue eyes. He wiped grease from the corners of his mouth.

"You, Songman, would throw a feast immediately if a scrap of food was brought to the village. I hope you have soothed the spirits, as killing wolves displeases them."

The speaker was an old, crooked little man with hair like a thick, silvery mane and yellow eyes which twinkled with hidden knowledge. He wore a wolf's coat and whenever he moved or was touched by a breeze, there was a faint rattle caused by the countless bones and teeth hanging from his garments. He was the only one who hadn't taken part in ripping the moose carcass apart, as if it wasn't appropriate for his silent dignity.

"Where did you find the woman?" he continued, having noticed Vierra, who stood a bit further away. The old man bowed to the woman, as per the old custom, and smiled.

"Worthy Runtamoinen, wolves tried to take our game, and we felled them in the middle of the onslaught. I soothed the spirits as you have taught me," replied Ulva to the old man, keeping his head low to honor him. "I wouldn't have taken the furs or the meat if our plight had not been so great. We stand on the brink of starvation and must do all we can to survive. Vierra, on the other hand," he pointed at the woman standing further away, "felled the moose that we had been following for half a day. We promised her a week's share of the carcass, as that is the hunter's right. She helped us to bring the moose here, saved me from a wolf's fangs and killed many of them. We should at least offer her the sweat hut before she continues her journey, wherever she is headed."

Runtamoinen walked to the woman and looked intensely into her eyes for a moment. She didn't dodge the gaze.

"You are of the wolf's blood and kin to her tribe. You can stay for the day and longer, too if you want to. Maybe you can even put some meat to dry, if you know how to do it."

"She is of chieftain's blood. Maybe she could lead us, like in the olden days, and come up with a plan to get our women and children back," Armas said, gazing at Vierra with a great deal of admiration in his eyes.

"I, for one, will not submit to your old ways anymore," stated Songman. "Maybe she can teach us to dry meat, but after that, we don't need her anymore. We will get your women back without an outsider's help. Or is it that you have been bowing to women so long that you can't do anything yourselves? If needs be, we'll steal women from another village to carry our children and clean our dwellings. You would break all the old rules and do the women's work, if somebody would hand it to you," snorted the old man. "Now, prepare the sweat hut for our young hunters and our guest."

The hut was made ready to warm up the freezing hunters. In the middle was a large heap of rocks, and, underneath them, wood was burned for a good while. Once the rocks had heated up, the fire was allowed to wane. The rocks then kept the hut heated nicely. The floor was covered with sprigs and dry hay. Planks cut from tree-trunks had been laid around the rocks for sitting purposes. Throwing water on the rocks increased the feeling of heat, and the most respected of the sauna-goers was chosen to throw the water. The hunters were always first to go in. Others entered in age order, with the eldest going first. Infants did not go into the sauna at all, except when they were given a name, and the bigger children were allowed to go after the adults, if there was still any heat left. There were no children in the village now, and so few adults left to enter the sauna as a group that the stones would have plenty of heat for everyone.

Vierra went with the hunters, although men and women used to go to the sauna together only on special occasions. The young men were shy about stripping naked in front of a stranger but Vierra did not mind and, outside the hut, she removed the wet clothes shrouding her skinny frame. After so many hungry months, there was little left of her impressive stature. Marks from the time she had spent as a Vikings' slave were everywhere on her body: countless spots where whip, lash or stick had bitten into her skin. She would carry the scars with her all the way to her funeral pyre. Even so, she was the only woman in this village of men and she felt their burning eyes in her back as she disrobed.

Swiftly, Vierra entered the hut and took her place by the pail of water. She opened her tight braid and let her dark mane spread like a black cloud around her head. With her hair loose, she looked more compassionate, and her green eyes glowed warmly in the light of the shingle. The young ones also stepped inside and seated themselves near the entrance.

Vierra struck the first water onto the rocks and a blissful warmth started to spread to the frost-numbed limbs of the hunters.

"What happened to your women, Ulva? You told me that you haven't seen them since last summer," Vierra asked, stretching her flexible limbs in the warmth, like a lynx in the morning sun.

"Tall bastards came last spring, when we were hunting. They killed all the men that had stayed in the village. We do not know what happened to our women and children. The raiders probably took them. We followed their trail until a great storm forced us to stop and ruined the tracks. We had no other option but to come back to the village." There was a glimpse of bitterness in Ulva's eyes.

"How do you know what the pillagers looked like?" asked Vierra.

"Runtamoinen told us they were tall men. Southerners," Ulva replied.

"So they can be of any tribe," Raito interrupted.

"Do not disturb the peace of the sauna," snorted Armas and rubbed his toes. They were always cold in the winter, no matter how good his fur shoes were.

The conversation faded as they threw more water, increasing the warmth. Finally, Vierra cast so much water onto the stones that everyone had to escape the heat by running into the snow outside.

"How odd this is. First, you are cold to the bone and then suddenly, it is so warm that you can't handle that, either," said Ulva. His eyes shone feverishly but he seemed to be in good health. They had to drink some snow-melt to quench their thirst, as there was nothing else to drink.

"Shall we try again?" Ulva suggested.

They returned to the darkness of the sweat hut. As Vierra threw the first scoop of water onto the rocks, the doorway opened. It was Songman, who entered without a word and sat down on a plank. He had already removed the clothes from his skinny frame and his haggard, white skin glowed in the shingle's light.

"Apparently, Songman doesn't care about the hunters' sauna peace, even though skis did not make their way to his feet, or a bow to his back," Ulva mused.

"Old hags' rantings," Songman answered. "If there's room on the planks, you can take your place." He looked at Vierra in the fluttering light with no shame. "What if I take you as my woman? You could bear my children and dry my fish and sweep my house. You would be wife to a great and wise man."

Vierra's soul was boiling, but she kept it out of her voice.

"I've let greater men than you pass by. The master of a pesky village, you say, but only tall men here bow to you. In place of women, you try to keep control here. How about this: I will keep throwing the water onto the stones and, if I leave first, I will stay here as your obedient wife. But if you go first, you will be under my rule, like men in the good old times, and I will do to you what I please. The rest of you can be the witnesses to our bet."

This idea came as a surprise to the men and Songman pondered over his decision over for a long time. Vierra's green eyes glowed, challenging the man, and there was a mischievous grin on her face.

"So be it," he finally stated. "You others, get out and we'll see who leaves first. I am no newcomer to the sweat hut."

Ulva left the hut with his companions and Armas, fast-tongued as always, quickly yelled the news for the other villagers to hear. Soon, everyone had gathered around the hut to await the result. Now and then, there was an angry hissing noise as water hit the rocks, but otherwise it was silent in the sauna. This continued for a while and the day stretched toward evening as the villagers waited. It was if nature itself was holding its breath and waiting for the result of this exciting match. Finally, two shapes staggered out of the hut, Songman foremost. Both stumbled onto the snow and took a heavy breath, as sweat beaded on their reddened skin. Vierra vomited heavily, throwing up the meal of venison she had had in the morning. She had lasted longest, and there was a victorious smile on her tired face.

"Cook enough meat for everyone to eat. The rest, I will hang out to dry. The wolf meat will be charred black on the fire and will be eaten from tomorrow on, until the dried meat is ready. Those in good health will go hunting tomorrow, as we will not survive long with this food." Vierra gave her orders while still lying in the ground, and the villagers obeyed; short men from old habit and tall ones reluctantly, reeling from their leader's defeat. There was a clearly visible smile on Runtamoinen's face as he left, even though he probably wouldn't participate in eating the wolf meat as the woman had ordered.

The cooking fire was soon lit and they started to cook the best cuts of the moose over it. A slaughter soup was made, in a big clay pot, out of the intestines and fat, while the bones and tendons of the animal were carefully gathered together. Vierra handled the drying of the meat. It was cut into pieces and laid out on a pallet beside a hut, where it would be exposed to the sun and the wind. The wolf pelts were prepared and their meat cooked by the fire, but Runtamoinen and Ulva wouldn't touch it. The wintry night darkened fast and the cold strengthened its grip. The half-moon and bright stars illuminated the area outside the campfire, turning the snow, which looked white in the daylight, into a deep blue expanse.

Songman stood with Raito and four other men, a bit further away. His expression was dark, and only a grueling hunger forced him to participate in the feast. The rest of the village gathered around Runtamoinen, his gang being stronger than Songman's by one man. The villagers couldn't have been more divided, with the tall men joining Songman and the short ones joining ranks with Runtamoinen.

Everyone filled their stomachs with soup and meat and the hunters had to describe the last two days' events so many times, they got tired. Runtamoinen took out his drum, made of wolf skin and bones, and started to pound it with a polished piece of bone. The even, hypnotic rhythm was catching and soon even Vierra noticed that she was nodding to it. Ulva started to sing with a low, sonorous voice. His eyes burned feverishly and sweat flowed down his forehead, even though it was very cold. Runtamoinen also joined in the singing with his own croaking voice. Vierra did not hear all the words accurately but one verse seemed to be recurring time and time again.

Hairy wolf, beast of forest
Wanderer so gray
Let me pass you in the dark wood
Do not pick me as your prey

We felled your kind, we slew your friend
Only in our dire need
So us men of lesser spirit
Could get our wretched feed

Songman stood up after he had eaten and started to walk toward an-
other lean-to. His men also got up, intending to follow their leader.
Ulva stopped singing and demanded furiously, "Where are you going?
It is not appropriate to leave during the holy song!"

"We go where we go, the eating is done and we don't care about
your songs," Raito answered.

"You southern brats don't honor anything or anyone, but you will
learn," Ulva replied ominously.

He got up, enraged. His eyes glowed in the campfire like a bright
yellow flame as he attacked Raito with one agile jump. The man was
caught completely off-guard and had no time to react whatsoever.
Ulva's fist found its way to Raito's cheek, throwing him down to the
snow. Ulva stormed on top of the fallen man, pounding him mind-
lessly with both fists. His rage was accompanied by a low, guttural
sound that came from deep within his throat. The villagers, witness-
ing this event, were dumbfounded, so sudden and violent had Ulva's
outburst been.

Vierra rose to the occasion quickly and rushed to pull Ulva away
from Raito, trying to calm him down. To her surprise, he jumped
up and grabbed her throat with both hands. There was a mindless,
sightless expression on the man's face and Vierra felt how his strong
grip started to squeeze with crushing strength.

Vierra reacted instinctively; her right knee jerked up and sank into
her opponent's crotch with a crunch. All the force of her short frame
was behind the kick. Ulva bent from the blow like a broken straw,

rolling on the ground in agony. He whimpered like a beaten dog, but an angry, bestial fire still burned in his eyes.

Vierra let her stare circle on the frozen villagers, her green eyes allowing no argument.

"This fight ends here! You will all die unless you learn to work together. A farmer or a hunter, you're both equally useless if you're dead."

Songman looked at her with open hostility. "We will see. Keep your dogs on the leash!"

Songman's men lifted up Raito, who was still lying prone and bleeding, and walked him back to his lean-to. The tall men disappeared behind its blackened entrance flap. Runtamoinen's group was left alone by the fading fire.

"Let's go inside too," Runtamoinen stated. "There's nothing more we can do today. Carry Ulva to the lean-to and we'll take care of him."

"Why did he attack me?" Vierra asked, as they dragged the slowly recovering Ulva toward his lean-to dwelling.

"The spirit of the wolf enters him from time to time, and it is up to me to persuade it out. You'll see. Keep your wits about you when you're with him."

"A wolf bit him while we were hunting."

"The spirit enters more easily from a wound. It gives him strength though, and heals his wounds quickly, but he has no control over it yet. He still has a lot to learn."

Ulva's gaze was threatening but he didn't try anything as the men carried him into the gloom of his abode.

The logs of the makeshift house were blackened on the inside. A crude fireplace and an opening for smoke had been created at one end and smoke could snake around the building to blacken the wood. The walls were patched with moss and the hard-trodden floor had been covered with straw. This was not the work of a master builder and the embers on the fireplace had to be properly set ablaze, if the men were to have warmth inside it.

Once the fire had been lit, Runtamoinen went close to it and a few men carried Ulva to him. The old man took his drum out again and started to beat it. This time, the rhythm was slower and more primal and neither he nor anyone else sang to it. Vierra took a step backwards and pulled Armas with her to the back of the lean-to. They wrapped themselves in pelts, side by side. The others were concentrated on the ritual that was taking place by Runtamoinen's fire.

"Where did Songman come from?" Vierra asked. She instinctively and gently stroked the boy's hair.

"Last winter, when there was a severe freeze, he came with his men, three cows and a few sacks of grain. Ulva's wife, Ranna, was our chieftain then, and she welcomed the travelers to our winter camp. At first, Songman pretended to be a good man, teaching us new songs and obeying when the women gave orders. Soon, however, his real nature started to show and since the spring's events, he and Runtamoinen have turned against each other. In the beginning, many of us rallied behind him. He taught us how to slash-and-burn and to build these houses. In the end, his clearance yielded little, and he couldn't preserve game like the women had. With winter came hunger and, as Songman isn't a good hunter either, only his own men listen to him now."

Runtamoinen's drumming strengthened and he let out low, guttural sounds to the rhythm of the drum. The crowd was completely focused on the ceremony.

"Runtamoinen blames Songman for stealing the women. He says we wouldn't have been surprised by the raiders if we had gone for the spring hunt, like the old customs say, and not stayed put like we are doing now." Armas glanced at Ulva. "Ulva has not been himself since his wife was taken. Sometimes I'm afraid of him." The boy shuddered.

Vierra pulled the boy closer and he started to doze. A year or two later, or in slightly different circumstances, their meeting under the hides would have been different. Now, he only clutched her as if she was his absent mother.

121

"We will talk sense to them tomorrow. If we can't get people to work together, everyone here will starve soon. Sleep now," Vierra tried to encourage the boy.

"The cows and the little crops we had left are all eaten, and so are the lingonberries. That moose won't keep us alive forever, so something has to be done soon," Armas said wearily.

Runtamoinen's session soon ceased and he looked happy. Ulva slept with heavy snores by the fireplace. For a moment, Vierra listened to the peaceful breathing of the boy sleeping next to her. She pulled more skins on top of them, to keep them warm. A strong human scent was mixed with that of smoke and, momentarily, Vierra missed sleeping alone, under open sky. The house was very warm, though, and she quickly fell asleep as the firewood crackled at the back of the fireplace, while the frost snapped on the outsides of the log walls.

A Dark Song on the Snow

It was the break of dawn when Vierra stuck her head out of the lean-to house. It wasn't long before she went back and yelled to the sleeping men. "Somebody has stolen the meat! There is not a single piece left."

Sleep was quickly shaken from the men's eyes and they hurried outside. The snowfall grew heavier by the minute as they wandered around, searching. All the meat, including that which Vierra had set to dry, was gone.

"The spirit of the wolf has punished us," was Runtamoinen's opinion. "We have to soothe the spirits to get the moose back."

"If the wolf spirit hasn't suddenly learned how to ski, we shall have to search for the perpetrator somewhere else," yelled Armas, coming from the outskirts of the village. "Six pairs of skis are missing. Songman's group is nowhere to be seen and there's a trail of a sledge and skiers that goes south."

The villagers quickly gathered to confer about what to do next.

"We should take our skis and go after them in numbers, they can't have got far," said Vierra. "Songman betrayed the promise he gave when we made our bet, and we have to get the meat back, in any case."

"My hunting and skiing days are long over, but there are other ways," said Runtamoinen and went into his hut. Nobody was allowed to follow him there and soon, the sounds of hollow drumming and coarse singing echoed from his dwelling.

As nobody had a better idea, the men quickly gathered their gear and got on their skis. Vierra led the group, along with the sharp-eyed Armas. Ulva was also with them but he remained silent. They started moving at once, but the journey progressed slowly due to the heavy snowfall, and the group had to stay very close together so as not to get separated from each other and become lost.

"The trail weakens, as if they were skiing on light snow and most of it only fell after they had passed," blurted Armas, visibly distressed and poking the trail with his spear.

"Songman's tricks, probably, but I will show him," said Ulva, breaking the silence and patting the end of his spear.

"We will carry on, there's not much choice," Vierra interrupted.

The snowfall got heavier, until the trail was impossible to see. The group, clueless, stopped to ponder about the next move.

"We should keep on going south. That's where they are going, anyway, to Songman's homelands," mused Armas.

"The trail will fade again, just like the trail of the ones that stole our women. This time, I won't go home until they've been caught." There was harsh bitterness in Ulva's voice.

"Look!" yelled Vierra, interrupting their contemplating.

The falling snow reduced visibility to a white-gray mist, but, at the edge of their vision, was a great, silver-maned wolf. It looked keenly at them and when Vierra walked towards it, it stood up and trotted further away. Then it sat again, looking at them as if waiting for someone to approach.

"Wolf brings good luck," said Ulva. "Let's follow it."

"I haven't seen any of that good luck here," Vierra snapped. She didn't have a better idea, though, so they let the wolf lead them into the thick snowfall.

Finally, the snowstorm started to ease up, and they could see their surroundings again. The escapees' trail was clearer now and the pursuers increased their pace, vitalized by the turn of their fortune. And so it was that, in a great, snow-covered glade, they finally caught the fugitives. There were six men, with a sledge on which the meat and goods were packed.

Vierra yelled at them from the edge of the opening.

"Halt! You like to eat venison and haul it away, too but you won't ski after it in the forest. Besides, you promised to obey me and submit to my will when you lost the bet in the sauna."

"If you give us the moose, you can go," added Armas.

Vierra placed a calming hand on the boy's shoulder. "Be careful, and stay beside me."

Songman turned, and the others stopped as well. It was then that they saw a sword on his belt. It was a rare sight, and a valuable weapon. Its price would have fed the whole group for a long time.

Ulva skied straight to Songman, yelling, "Will you give me the meat, or shall I beat you like I beat your slave yesterday? Nobody's going to help you now."

What followed would have been beautiful, had it not been so violent. Songman unsheathed his sword and struck in one perfectly smooth motion. Gracefully, like a snake, the weapon swung through the air and severed Ulva's head from his shoulders, spraying blood all over the surrounding snow. Songman's white hair fluttered and his ice-blue eyes burned triumphantly.

"Come and try your luck. The Blood Drinker calls its own. The moose you will get only over my stiff, cold body."

This horrible act wiped away all possibility of negotiation and the long-smoldering discord burst into a devastating flame. First, it was arrows that flew between the enemies. The pursuers were still amongst the trees and so had better cover from the shooting. Two of Songman's men fell from the arrows, and one of Vierra's group.

Vierra followed the shooting from her shelter, taking no part in it. This fight, if any, was mindless and in vain.

"Armas, don't go!" Vierra yelled, but it was too late. The eager boy left the shelter of the trees during a lull in the rain of arrows and attacked Songman. He thrust his spear toward Songman's chest but the man dodged and swiped diagonally down with his sword. The boy collapsed and the snow beneath him flooded red with blood. Vierra's hopes of a rational future were buried in bloody snow. Her bow fired an arrow toward Songman, who was standing alone. He was an easy target, as he just stood there with no intention of running for cover. He laughed and sang loudly.

> *I know now the birth of bow*
> *Singing the song of death*
> *Arrow will not touch the Songman*
> *Draw my blood or breath*

To her surprise, Vierra saw that her arrow had clearly missed its mark. Annoyed, she notched another arrow. This time she aimed carefully before the shot, until she was absolutely sure that it would hit home. Again, the result was to disappoint her; the arrow passed its target, although only just. Songman flinched and looked at Vierra. The over-confidence that had been in his eyes before was gone now and he ordered his three remaining men to charge. Runtamoinen's group faced them. The melee was clumsy in the snow as everyone was fighting on their skis.

Vierra dropped the bow and grabbed the same broad-headed spear she had used as a ski-pole. It was heavy and clumsy for throwing but she nevertheless hurled it towards Songman. He dodged the incoming spear and skied toward Vierra, the blood of Ulva and Armas trickling from his sword.

"Even though you can't be hit with an arrow, you have to dodge the spear," Vierra mocked. However, the only weapon she now had left was her scramasax with a cubit-length blade, which she pulled out in order to face the man.

It was an uneven battle. Vierra's blade was shorter than Songman's and the man was much taller than her. She swung her weapon at the approaching man but he easily parried the blow and struck the blade from her hands, sending it far away into the snow. He raised his sword to strike and burst out laughing.

"I will take your head back home and ask it for permission for my acts. This is my way of keeping my promise to you."

The sword rose and Vierra prepared to make a desperate dodge, but the blow was never delivered. A great, silver-maned wolf jumped at Songman and both the animal and the man fell to the snow. There, they wrestled each other until Songman managed to pull a knife from his belt. A few fast stabs and the wolf yelped, jumping away. It dragged itself on the snow, staining the perfect white with a trail of blood, until it finally slumped, remaining completely still.

Songman took his eyes off the wolf only to see Vierra standing over him, her bow drawn and an arrow only half a meter away from his face.

"Sing this away," Vierra said and released the arrow. And Songman sang no more.

With the last, dying gaze of its glazed eyes, the great, silver-maned wolf watched the forest glade, which had turned into a battlefield. Only a black-haired woman moved in the field, looking for any survivors among the fallen. When she found none, she skied to the sledge full of venison and filled her backpack with meat.

What the wolf's eyes didn't get to see was the woman stopping by the corpse of a young, blond boy. They didn't notice her sad look as she closed the boy's eyes, which remained open in death.

And they didn't see how she started to ski toward the north, towards her homeland, with a brisk pace. She did not look back.

On Treacherous Ground

I N THE swamp you could still feel it. The cold grasp of winter, which was reluctantly leaving the northern lands. From amid twigs and moss, a cold, damp vapor rose to impede the three travelers who disturbed its peace. The first was a dark-haired man, his hands tied behind his back. The eyes of the prisoner were bleak and glassy, and he clearly didn't know where he was going. Behind him was a woman who jostled and prodded her prisoner in the desired direction. Her head was covered with a hood, and her face couldn't be seen in the dark, cloudy morning light. Behind these two came a sturdy, blond-haired man, who had an air of sluggishness about him as was often found with larger men. He kept some distance from the two that walked before him. The man was immensely strong; he was carrying a large stone in each hand without them appearing to affect his progress in any way.

No words were exchanged, and the trio walked in silence, concentrating on avoiding the morasses that crossed their path. The call of a lonely curlew echoed in the damp air. Many other birds hadn't yet returned to the northern swamps to spend the summer there. Some patches of snow still remained, like the last breaths of the resisting, dying winter.

The travelers arrived at a great quagmire. It was so wide that a grown man would have needed to make four leaps to cross it. There were no footholds for making those kinds of leaps, though, only the calm surface of the water, covered with a thin, grey layer of ice after the cold night. The woman yanked her prisoner to a halt and beckoned the man behind her to approach. She took the rocks that the strong man had been carrying and, with a rope that she'd been using as a belt, tied them to the dark-haired prisoner. He did nothing to stop her, just stood there as if in a trance. She yanked the hood off her head and her black hair flew free. With a strong voice, she sang:

> *Spirits of the gloomy swampland*
> *Little people in the deep*
> *Chorus of the helpless children*
> *Victims who the death will keep*
>
> *Hear me well, my offer take*
> *Down now pull him to you*
> *Eat him with your hungry mouths*
> *All blood, gut and sinew*
>
> *Give me luck and grant me hope*
> *Give me back what life did steal*
> *Though I come from world above you*
> *All my wounds and ailments heal*

The woman kicked her black-haired prisoner in the back, and he fell headfirst into the grey mire. The ice on the surface broke with a crack, and the victim sank like the rocks that had been attached to him. Only the faintest splash could be heard, and nothing could be seen on the surface other than a slowly drifting trail of bubbles. These subsided quickly, leaving only the broken ice on the surface as witness to the deed.

The woman and the man walked away from the swamp in silence. Perhaps the mist that the swamp raised was a bit thicker than before. Perhaps the peat mosses' squelch was livelier, or the waters in the quagmire glimmered more brightly than before. The woman pulled the hood back over her head after combing her black hair back with her fingers. Only one wisp of hair, white like the flowers of wild rosemary, stayed, curled on her forehead, as if against her will.

The Survivor

One step, then another. At first, when Vierra had fallen sick, she had counted the days until the fever would let go. After it had gotten worse, she had counted the hours of the day and counted each stick of firewood as she collected it with her fading strength, to make sure there would be sufficient for the coming night. Now, as she walked, she could only count steps, one at a time.

Those agonizing steps carried her through a forest that was freeing itself from winter. The melting snow had revealed brown-grey ground, which was waiting for warmth and light to green it up for its spring blossoming. Shadowy spots were covered here and there with odd-shaped patches of snow, which were fighting a losing battle against the approaching summer. And even though the summer in the north was short, it would inevitably come, just like every year before this one.

Vierra followed a trail that hunters had trampled down. Every sound of the surrounding forest was familiar to her, its lights and shadows like invitations to a traveler who had been away from home for a long time. If she had been in full strength, the sense of her homeland would have surely made her mistreated heart feel like bursting. Now, however, her eyes were fixed on the path before her. A single, pounding thought in her feverish head told her to take one step after another, toward the lands of her tribe.

Vierra was a master at surviving in the wild, even by the standards of her own people, hardened hunter-gatherers though they were. Still, being alone in the wilderness was going to kill her eventually. During the wet snows of the period between winter and spring, the wisp's disease had gotten in her. Only when she had realized that she couldn't survive without the help of others, had she set off to look for the people of her tribe. The northern forests and swamps were vast, though, and her tribe would be constantly on the move now that the snows were melting. Vierra earnestly hoped that her tribe members hadn't yet left for the coast, for the spring trading. With her diminishing strength, she wouldn't make it there.

Vierra snapped awake from her slumber. She had fallen down on all fours, and felt the cold surface of snow against her burning cheek. It had happened many times before, and she had always gotten up to continue her journey. Now, the cool snow felt tempting: maybe she would sleep for just a moment, gather strength and then continue on her way. With a creak, Vierra clenched her teeth, trying to subdue this whispering voice inside her.

The voice of her inner struggle was quenched, not by her tenacity but by another's voice that reached her ears from the forest trail as she lay down. Her sharp ears made no mistake, even with the fever: she was sure there were hunters of her tribe coming along the trail, maybe to check their traps. The last vestiges of strength left Vierra's limbs. She had longed for this meeting for so many days, counted her steps and made her pain-filled mind believe that she would make it back to her people. Now that her objective was about to be met, her tormented body couldn't give her any more.

Vierra stood at the swamp. The breeze of early spring blew onto her back, and she shivered from the cold. Somewhere, a curlew let out its melancholic call. There were no smells of the swamp in the air; the ground was hard against her feet, as if frozen. In the reddened light of the sun that was setting on the horizon, Vierra saw a large quagmire. Its surface was black and immobile. It emanated coldness and she instinctively took a step backwards.

Only then did she notice the black-haired woman that stood beside her. She was gazing into the distance, and Vierra couldn't distinguish her face even when she tried to look as sharply as possible. The woman slowly stepped into the mire, and the black water gradually engulfed her. Cold wind blew her black hair, amid which Vierra could see a few white wisps.

Vierra, shivering from the cold, was filled with horror. She wanted to help this woman, to pull her away from the cold and the death she faced, but her legs felt rooted to the spot and she could do nothing but watch. The faceless woman sank into the water, first up to her hips, then all the way up to her neck. The woman turned to her, and Vierra still couldn't see her face. She knew one thing, though, sensing it rather than seeing it; the faceless woman was smiling.

Vierra returned to her senses in complete darkness. With strength borne of the nightmare, she tried to get up, but weakness forced her to close her eyes and take a deep breath. Her head was spinning and she felt a hollow, metallic nausea in her stomach. But she felt warm. Thick bed skins had been tightly wrapped around her, and the air smelled of fire-smoke.

A wedge of light punctured Vierra's darkened world as someone opened the entrance skin of the hut. In the dark, she could distinguish red hair and the profile of round cheeks. She would have recognized her old friend Rika even after a lifetime of slavery. When Rika realized Vierra was trying to get up, she hurried to push her back down. The women hugged each other for a long time. Finally, Rika huffed loudly and pulled back.

"Don't try to get up, just rest." Rika accidentally touched one of Vierra's scars, which ran from her chest to her shoulder, and pulled her hand back.

Vierra grimaced. "They don't hurt anymore, they healed a long time ago."

"Can you eat? I have some trout broth. Eera says that we can't give you any solid food yet."

No force in the world could have made Vierra decline the food. Even the thought of eating caused a painful feeling of emptiness in the pit of her stomach.

"I can eat."

Rika set a wooden cup to her lips and Vierra grabbed it with both hands, gulping down the broth in huge mouthfuls.

"Easy, easy. Otherwise you'll throw everything up, and we haven't gotten anywhere. There, now you have to sleep. Eera and I shall thank the spirits that we got you back. We all thought you were dead."

"I've slept enough. And don't bother the spirits on my account. Help me up, I want to breathe the air outside."

Confused, Rika wrinkled her brow. She did as her friend asked, though, and soon they stepped out of the hut together. The spring sun blinded Vierra's eyes mercilessly, and for a long time she stood outside the hut to get her eyes accustomed to the light. The patches of snow had lost their battle against the summer. It was the moment in spring that felt as if everything stood still. The deciduous trees waited, the buds on their branches ready to sprout. The whole of nature was full of coiled strength, just waiting for the sun's warmth in order to be unleashed.

The whole tribe, along with the elderly and the children, gathered around Vierra. She remembered leaving a larger tribe than this one she had returned to. The ones that remained looked ragged. If Vierra's life had been hard, her relatives hadn't had it easy, either. Vierra's sudden appearance had been like rejuvenating water to the people who had wilted under their burden. Questions were flying in the air like raindrops in a thunderstorm, and because of their torrent she couldn't answer any of them.

"Let her be!" yelled Eera, who arrived, swaying. Her hair had gotten even whiter and she had to rely on a cane to stay on her feet. The eyes, flaring deep in their sockets, hadn't weakened though. "Vierra shall tell her story as soon as she feels able. Until then, leave her alone."

"I can do it, but give me something to eat. The trout broth won't soothe my hunger."

"You can't eat yet," Rika interrupted. "Your stomach can't handle stronger food yet."

Eera looked at Vierra, assessing her from under her brow. "Let her eat. Give her food."

With an eagerness that burned with curiosity, the tribe prepared a feast for Vierra. There was fried trout, venison jerky and the first wild-plants of the year, making a meal tasty enough to tempt anyone. And Vierra ate like a starving woman. Twenty pairs of eyes watched her every move, longing for the meal to end and the story to begin.

So, after eating, Vierra started to speak. She told of the baleful day of the fire festival, of her fight with the invaders, of slavery and all the strange things she had experienced. She told of her journey through the forests and the moose hunt that had ended in the deaths of many men. She told of the harsh winter, too, and what had almost happened to her with the disease.

"The spirits have been in your favor, for, after all of these ordeals, you are still alive," Eera blurted out, when the long story had come to an end.

"I feel like it's the spirits themselves that keep causing me trouble, hardship and sorrow, and that I have to overcome them with my own strength. Did the spirits help me when my son and husband were slain? Did they brush honey on these lash marks when I was a slave to the intruders? Did they help me in my battle against Songman? Yes, the spirits have cursed me over and over again, but from now on I will curse them back." Vierra's green eyes burned, and she sang:

> *Seita-stone, you dog's bone*
> *Spirits big and small*
> *I won't fear your wretched warnings*
> *I won't hear your call*
>
> *Try to meddle, try to settle*
> *Do your worst to me*
> *I cut your trees, ignore your fees*
> *You can't my fate foresee*

Other tribe members listened to the mocking song, horrified, and many made a gesture to protect them from evil.

"Stop this defiance at once! I understand that you have suffered a lot, and you want to find someone to blame for it, but this is not the right way. It is even worse that you chose to do so now." Eera spread her arms out toward the members of the tribe that sat beside her. "Is our tribe strong? The wisp's disease and the southerners have taken half of us."

Vierra's expression didn't change.

"Because you and Rika have healed me, I will obey your word. But my mind will not be easily changed."

"Many of those that you don't see sitting here by the fire, have been taken away by the wisp's disease. The very same that burned inside you. Still, when I asked the spirits of the plants to heal you, they bestowed it. Even though they've been silent when so many others have fallen ill and died. You should thank them, not reproach them."

Vierra sat silently and thought about the words Eera had spoken to her. The tribe members were suddenly in a hurry to get back to their chores, wherever they might be. So it was that they were reminded that this woman was the Fargoer, and the years hadn't changed that.

Rika looked sad, and Vierra looked at her old friend and softened her expression slightly, saying, "Very well, I apologize for my words. My life hasn't been easy. Every day since my son went to the Underworld has been dark. Only defiance has kept me alive. Here in my homeland, though, the sun warms me from the inside. Tell me everything that has happened while I have been away."

And Rika told her. She told of the lean years, of how she had found a man from the winter camp and had a son. They had both died of the disease last fall. The whole tribe had been afflicted by a serious wisp fever, and not only them but other members of the Kainu, too. Rika, who was usually a happy soul, had a grim expression on her face.

"And the disease didn't spare the chieftain, either. All of Aure's daughters fell ill and died, one after another. And then her husbands, two out of three were lost. Only the oldest and strongest, Kaira, was left alive."

Vierra listened thoughtfully. "Did my cousin go to the Underworld, too?"

"No, the spirits saved her. Even so … I wouldn't say it to her out loud." Rika lowered her voice. Vierra could not remember ever having seeing her friend scared like that. "She buried her family in the swamp herself. She buried them like old witches were buried once, without burning. Eera tried to stop her, but Aure was distraught with sorrow. I've never seen her like that. And after that ..."

"Where is she now?" Vierra interrupted and looked around, searching for Aure.

"As if it was not enough that the disease has thinned our numbers and the spirits have been silent, the southern hay-biting fur traders have started to steal furs during the last few years, and last spring they came with large groups of men and attacked our unsuspecting sisters. Many Kainu died, and they took women with them to the south, as prisoners. And they didn't burn the bodies of those they killed, but left them to rot, desecrated."

"But where is Aure?" Vierra asked, with a hint of impatience in her voice.

Rika smiled pallidly. "Be patient and I'll tell you. Aure summoned a great gathering, all of the Kainu. She's planning a war expedition against the southerners. They are probably on their way here right now, now that the smiling sun has driven away the ice. Eera tried to talk to her, suggesting that perhaps we should wait another spring and build up our defenses. But Aure had made her decision."

"I, too, have seen what the southerners can do. Maybe I would have done the same, had I been in Aure's position."

Rika had no time to answer, because the tribe members that had escaped Vierra's outburst silently returned to the village square. The reason for their return soon became obvious when the grim-faced chieftain of the tribe emerged from the forest.

Campfire Council

The spring evening was rapidly darkening into a pitch-black night. The fires lit by the Kainu reflected a play of flickering lights and shadows onto the faces of those who were sitting in a ring around the flames. Aure stood in the center of the ring, close to the fire. The red of the flames played with her hard features as she explained what had happened at the gathering. The hood she had pulled over her head highlighted the furrows of her face.

"The great women of the Kainu were in discord, as you guessed," Aure said, pointing to Rika. "And, by following your advice, I persuaded them to stand with me."

Aure took a small break.

"The speaker for our southern tribes is a man," she continued.

"I told you it would be so," Rika said, with a smile in her eyes; a smile which didn't reach her face.

Eera wasn't a member of the council. It was rumored that she would leave for her final journey this summer, and appoint Rika to replace her.

"You'll become a witch one of these days, as long as the war party proves to be successful," Aure replied. "I will take two hunters with me. We will unite with the others and make the dishonorable southerners fear our forests."

Aure let her eyes move around the people of her tribe; people whose numbers had been depleted by disease and hunger. There weren't many young, eager faces amongst them.

"Kaira," Aure said, and an immensely strong man stepped toward his wife in the center of the ring. "Who else wants to come?"

"I want to break southerners' skulls," a tall young man blurted, squeezing his hands into fists.

"Any other volunteers beside Kaarto?" Aure asked. "Even though you're eager, you're too young and inexperienced for a hunting trip like this. And we may not return from this journey. We have so few of you young ones." The expression on the face of the grim chieftain was darker than ever.

The silence was broken only by the crackling of firewood in the campfire. These tribe members, who had suffered so much, just wanted to move to the places of the fire festival and the rising salmon of the summer. The war party was like a torn moose skin to their normal circle of life.

"I can go with you." The owner of this deep and sonorous voice stepped confidently beside Aure and Kaira, even though Aure hadn't chosen her yet.

Rika's eyes widened with surprise. She quickly gathered her wits, though. "Vierra, you cannot go to war, you are sick," she insisted.

Aure put her hand on her cousin's shoulder. The gesture was warm, but Vierra felt nothing behind it. She remembered Aure as she had always been: sparkly, like a campfire made of spruce. Now, the chieftain exuded coldness and indifference. The person who stood beside her was unknown to Vierra. The old Aure would have surely made her opinion known to all.

"If there are no other volunteers, get the gathering rocks. Let the will of the tribe decide who should go and who should stay."

It was done, and more wood was added to the central fire. By the light of the refreshed flames, the members of the tribe voted on who would go to war. Most didn't hesitate, and dropped their rocks straight into the jar. Rika's expression was grim as Aure poured the contents of the gathering jar into a brightly-lit spot near the fire.

Only one rock seconded Kaarto. Judging by the other votes, Vierra would be the one to go. The tribe spoke as if with one voice, and Rika's grief poured over.

"Why did you volunteer?" she yelled at Vierra, with a rare anger in her voice. "I thought that you were my friend, but it seems I was wrong." The red-haired woman turned around and disappeared into the dark with a strong, determined step.

"We leave at daybreak," Aure stated. Nothing about her gave away what she thought about the incident, but the color of her rock, as well as those of the tribe, was clear.

Vierra shaded her eyes from the rising sun. It was engulfed by a light curtain of clouds that colored the light blood red. Squinting her eyes,

Vierra looked toward a high hill atop of which a funeral was taking place.

All of the Kainu had gathered there, and Vierra climbed to the top of the hill among the others. The fire burned fiercely, and it was not possible to recognize the deceased as the body was already engulfed by the flames. Everyone stood there in silence. Someone should have recited the funeral words, but nobody did a thing. Vierra looked at the expressionless, sorrowful faces of her fellow tribe members. None of them looked back. She tried to sing on their behalf, but nobody listened, and her voice disappeared into the wind.

A huge eagle approached from the east, as if emerging straight from the rising sun. The light glowed on the tips of its wings as it came, gliding majestically toward the funeral party. Skillfully and calmly, it circled down and snatched the deceased with its talons from amid the fire, like its earthly brother would have taken a hare.

Turmoil took over the tribe. If they were silent before, now they yelled together at the top of their voices and ran down from the hill, any way they could. Vierra clapped her hands over her ears. The eagle had disappeared back to where it had come from, with its prey.

Vierra snapped awake. Anxiety burned in her chest, and bad thoughts rose to trouble her from every direction. Her body, weakened by the long illness, screamed for rest, but her restless mind didn't allow her to fall asleep again. She twisted and turned on her bed skin in the lone women's hut, and tried to push her mind and thoughts aside for long enough so she could catch some sleep.

Launi was snoring, just like she had done during those countless nights that Vierra had spent in the same hut as her, while she still resided with her tribe. Rika was nowhere to be seen, however. Since the family of the witch-to-be had died of disease, she, too, had been sleeping in the lone women's hut; and would continue to do so until receiving the witch's necklace, after which she would have a lean-to to herself.

Finally, Vierra got up, frustrated. If she couldn't sleep, she might as well go and look for Rika. Maybe she could make amends with her friend before leaving.

Almost impenetrable darkness greeted her beyond the door skin of the hut. The Kainu huts, along with the trees surrounding the camp, loomed black against the dark gray surroundings. Soon, the Kainu would leave to fish the salmon that rose to the streams in the summer, and after the fire festival they would again separate, along with their families, to fish and spend the last warm days of the summer resting and gathering strength to see them through the long autumn and winter.

The camp was silent, and indeed there was no reason to be moving around in the dark. The night birds of the summer didn't sing so early in spring, and the night was as silent as it was black.

Vierra sharpened her eyes to catch her surroundings. A few dogs lifted their ears as she moved, but didn't bark. She had spent enough time with the tribe for the animals to recognize her scent, and count her as one of the members.

Only red embers were left of the fire that had been burning in the center of the camp, and it brought a small, dim glow of light to the darkness. Vierra moved closer and soon heard the voices of women who were sitting there, talking quietly. She sneaked closer, not daring to interrupt their discussion.

"I am tired, both of dealing with all the ills and squabbles of the tribe, and of my own weakness. Besides, you take care of everything better than I can now. You don't need me anymore, I'm just a burden. You have gathered your necklace and I've taught you everything I know. It's time to summon the spirits to judge your next step."

The talker was Eera. Vierra saw only a hunched figure against the glow of the embers, but the voice of the old witch was unmistakable. So was the voice that answered the elder; it was the one which had spoken to Vierra last night in anger and disappointment. There was a similar bitterness present this time, as well.

"You can't leave now, when the fate of the chieftain and the future of our whole people are at stake while we go to war against the southerners. I can't persuade the spirits to be favorable in such great things. They haven't even accepted me yet."

"They will. Give me your necklace." The shapes moved against the weak glow of the embers. "This is finely made. Perfect. You have nothing to fear while carrying this on your neck."

"Then leave. Leave, all of you, die or leave!"

There was an angry determination in Rika's step as she swept through the opening. Even if the young witch had seen Vierra when she passed her, she didn't let it show.

Vierra emerged from her hideout. Eera's dark shape looked at her for a moment, but neither of them said anything. Soon, Vierra slipped back into her hut.

Vierra didn't get to see Rika before she left, as she kept away and didn't come to say goodbye to the three of them as they left at first light. Only later, while unpacking their food, Vierra found the necklace. And it was finely made, of countless teeth and bones of different animals. After a moment's hesitation, Vierra slipped it on her neck, and hid it under her furs.

Hatreð Flows Southwarð

The large gathering glade of the Kainu was full of people, for the second time that spring. At the center of the forest glade was the huge council stone, surrounded by white, old birches. The last time Aure had stepped on the stone, the birches had been bare. Now, they had conjured tiny leaf buds that framed the serious, hooded figure of the chieftain.

There were nearly a hundred listeners, the finest of all the tribes. Women and men, all wearing bows on their backs and knives on their belts. The southern Kainu were distinguishable by their clothing: in addition to skins, they had more wool and cloth, which they had made themselves or traded with Vikings and other southern people. The northernmost had painted their faces with blue patterns, in the old way of the Kainu when going to war. The group was a frightening sight to behold, and one didn't envy the raiders making their way up from the south, unaware of what they would be facing.

Aure whittled an arrow on the stone. After sharpening it, she lifted it high over her head and sang:

> *Straight is the arrow of war*
> *Bitter is the point of hate*
> *You are one among the many*
> *My enemy's last fate*
>
> *Fly as the wind, fly with my wrath*
> *Fly until the peace will come*
> *Shattered then will be your shaft*
> *Peace will boom the chieftain's drum*

Aure stepped down from the rock, and the whole group started to move southward, with no specific plan. On the well-trodden paths, the troop made good progress. Here and there, they saw fields and the group passed a group of winter houses in the distance. Scouts were chosen, and they went in every direction, probing the area and looking for signs of the southern people's bands.

In the evening, the group approached a great lake, the northern shore of which had traditionally been the southern part of the Kainu lands. Vierra had gone ahead of the main group, scouting, when human sounds carried to her ears. She sneaked closer and saw a group of ten men, sitting by a fire and roasting fish. The southerners' campfire still burnt brightly as the Kainu prepared to ambush them from every direction, from an arrow's distance.

There was no mercy. The Kainu worked as hunters, as always. More than twenty bows spoke their deadly words almost instantaneously. Most of the southerners fell on the spot. One young man fell face-first into the fire, which roused a cloud of sparks and filled the air with the stench of burning flesh. An older, grey-bearded man managed to run a few steps before falling down, impaled by multiple arrows. When all of them had fallen, the Kainu rushed from the forest like wolves and finished the job with their knives. The Kainu rarely went to war, and when they did, it wasn't a beautiful sight.

"We will escort them to the Underworld, like we would our own. We will do it tomorrow at sunrise. Now we shall camp here and sing to honor of their spirits." Aure organized her group and they slept in one huddle, with two guards posted at any given time. By the campfire, the Kainu quietly sang their songs of the Underworld. This was one of their ways to make sure that the ghosts of the slain southerners wouldn't come back, to avenge the wrong they had experienced.

Vierra woke before sunrise. The campfire still glowed, but the area was gloomy and silent. Vierra looked around and saw sleeping Kainu here and there, but no guards anywhere. While she was wondering, Aure and Kaira stepped from the forest. They sneaked back to the camp and started to build up the waning fire.

"What happened?" Vierra asked her cousin.

Aure looked surprised for a moment. "We heard noises from the forest and went to see. There was nothing there, though. You just go back to sleep." She resettled her hood on her head.

Here and there, some of the group woke up at the sound of talking, but, as the conversation ceased, they soon went back to sleep. Vierra lay back down, but could not shake off the feeling that something was not right and she couldn't sleep anymore.

The first rays of the rising sun fell upon a great funeral pyre. Large trees had been felled the previous evening, and they were now ignited from many spots with feather-sticks. The southerners' bodies had been piled on top of the trees, and there they burned, along with the wood. No more songs were sung and, when the Kainu moved out, only a funeral pyre was left, to burn in the middle of the forest.

The Kainu continued south, along the shores of the great lake. The boats of the slain southerners were put to use and rowed toward the south along the shoreline. Aure had divided her group in two: one moving through the forest on the eastern side under her command, while the other group went with Kirre on the western bank.

Kirre was the leader of the southern Kainu, a seasoned and cruel woman who was made for leading a war party. Only a few votes had separated Kirre and Aure when they had chosen the high chieftain to lead the group in the gathering.

Vierra was with Aure's group. Because of her sharp eyes, she had been put on one of the boats taken from the southerners. From there, she scanned the horizon, on the lookout for southern boats, should any appear. Kaira was rowing the boat, keeping its presence as imperceptible as possible by going through coves, reeds and gliding behind rocks. The Kainu knew that the southerners preferred to use boats, and kept roughly to the same routes every year. The boats made it easy and effortless to transport their stolen cargo back south.

"Look at those glades," Kaira stated after a long silence, and pointed his thick finger toward openings in the forest in the south. "The southern hay-biters have burned trees to make space for their hay crop. It will take a long time before a decent forest will grow there again."

"That's nothing. The invaders have burned even larger areas around their villages, so big that you couldn't shoot an arrow from one side to the other. They can stay at their houses for weeks and just work, without going to hunt or fish in between."

"They aren't real people, those Vikings. And our southern people are well on their way to becoming like them."

"Look!" Vierra interrupted their discussion and pointed at a boat that had been beached in one of the bays.

At the same moment, two men dashed from the forest as if evil spirits were after them. It was just as bad, as angry swarms of arrows, one after another, were shot from the forest. Some magic was protecting these southern men, for no arrow struck them, and they immediately pushed their boat into the water. An older, sturdy man went for the oars and rowed for his life. The boat glided out into the lake and was soon outside the reach of the arrows shot by the Kainu standing on the beach. A yell was heard from the shore.

"Vierra and Kaira, row after them and kill them, so they can't warn the others."

A rowing competition started on the lake, with a prize of life or death. The southern man pulled hard on the oars, making their boat fly towards the south and safety. But in the end, Kaira's oar pulls were longer. His arms, legs and back took turns to do the work and muscles bulged from wherever they showed under his leather garment. Slowly, inevitably, one pull at a time, the Kainu boat caught up on the escapees.

Vierra stood up on the speeding boat, bracing her legs against the sides, a deed that demonstrated considerable balance and mastery. She drew her bow and released after just a brief moment of aiming. An angry arrow darted from her weapon, striking its target with unfailing accuracy. The rower on the other boat collapsed, his heart impaled by the arrow. Without a rower, the boat quickly slowed down and was left adrift. Vierra drew another arrow to her bow, but didn't see the other man who had been on the boat.

"Kaira, row closer to the boat, carefully," she directed the rower, who slowly pulled the craft towards its goal.

The wind turned the southerners' boat and as they approached, Vierra and Kaira spotted the other man. He was crouched down in the bottom of the boat, showing no signs of resistance.

"Turn the aft toward it and row backwards, I'll go and see," Vierra whispered quietly. Kaira did so, and Vierra set down her bow. When the boats touched, she jumped lightly into the southerners' boat, with her scramasax in her hand. She yanked the crouching man up and got ready to thrust her blade into his throat.

Vierra's hand stopped, however, when she saw the man's face. A boy, barely ten summers old, stared back at her. The blond hair was stained with dirt and sweat, the young blue eyes were wide and full of panic. Inside Vierra rose a storm of conflicting forces. A voice said, "Kill the southerner. Even if it's not adult yet, it will soon be one, a fur collector. It won't thank you if you let it go, but it will kill you if it gets the opportunity." But even stronger was the voice that said, "It could be your son, if he was still alive. He's a little older but he has the same blond hair and blue eyes. So what if he's a southerner? Is he all that different? He's just a child." For a moment, Vierra struggled with herself about what to do.

She turned and rolled the dead man overboard into the water and jumped back into her own boat. Looking at the boy and pointing towards the south with her finger, she yelled frantically, "Go on! Row home while you still can!"

The boy was so shocked that he didn't immediately realize what was happening, but, after a moment, he stumbled to the rower's seat and started to pull the boat jerkily towards the south. Vierra looked at the moving boat for a moment, and then blurted, "They're even sending children to do their bidding! Row back to the shore."

Kaira didn't say anything, just pulled the oars. Vierra couldn't tell if he agreed with her or not. That was his nature; his emotions were hidden inside him so that nobody else could see them.

An argument quickly started with Aure on the shore about what had just happened.

"Why didn't you kill him? You even gave him a boat to travel in! He will surely warn all the others that come along," Aure said, with poison in her voice.

Anybody else would have been frightened in the face of the chieftain's anger. Vierra looked calm. If there was turmoil inside her, she didn't show it.

"He was just a boy. I won't kill children, southerners or not. I have seen enough children die for one lifetime. I will not kill any more of them, not even if my own life depended on it.

"You! You have been through such a lot, for you've lost one son." There was bitter sarcasm in the chieftain's voice. "I guided all three of my daughters to the Underworld last winter, while you sat inside a house in faraway lands. Two of my men, I buried in the same pile, and the third one seems useless, for he lets enemies escape." She leered towards Kaira, who was expressionless. "If any of us die because of this, their lives are on your soul. And if the hunt fails, we will never forgive you." Aure's face was like a petrified mask.

Vierra remained calm, adamant in her decision. Others were silent. Arguing with each other was unheard of in this situation, when everyone's life depended on their joint strength and determination. When the group started moving again, whispers passed between neighboring tribe members whenever they thought they would not be overheard by Aure or Vierra.

This time, Aure didn't order the bodies to be burned, but drove her troops south for the whole day until evening. As dusk set over the land, sounds of fighting could be heard from the other side of the lake. They looked across the water, but, in the dim light the moon threw down, even sharp-eyed Vierra couldn't see anything on the opposite shore. It soon became too dark to carry on and they had no choice but to stop for the night. They didn't light a fire, but spent the night sleeping side by side, sharing the warmth of each other's bodies.

The Siege

The trek resumed early in the morning. The war party reached the southern end of the lake and paused in a small, treeless glade. A broad, well-trodden path could be seen leading to the south. As they headed towards it, Kirre's group caught up with them on the edge of the glade. They had met a large group of southerners the previous night, and the battle that had broken out had claimed the lives of several Kainu. Only a few southerners had escaped their wrath and had run away, bloodied and bruised, to the south.

Now, an unknown land unfolded in front of them. The Kainu had fished in the great southern lake, but only a few older members of the southern Kainus had ever come this far. They stopped to discuss what to do next.

"Let's keep going south and burn everything in our path. That will teach them to stay in their own land," Kirre suggested. She had a bloody wound on her forehead from last night's battle, which made her old, hard face look even more brutal.

"That will drive them to seek vengeance, at least, and the southern Kainu will be the ones to suffer the brunt of their anger. It's best to just kill the patrols that move north," answered Bjorn, the speaker of southern tribes. He was a large man with lively eyes, and he was looked down on by the northern women.

"For such a big, strong man, you are quite a coward," Kirre snarled.

The blond man's eyes narrowed with anger, but Aure interrupted them. "Let's see what these southerners' lands are like. Then I'll decide what to do."

The chieftain's word was heeded, and the group continued, with the scouts moving ahead. They sneaked forward, on both sides of the path. This way, anyone coming down the trail wouldn't notice them. They didn't have to wander for long, for the path soon led into a clearing, where many log houses had been built beside a small creek. The Kainu observed it for a moment, from the shelter of the forest. Nothing could be seen moving and they slunk across the clearing and into the houses.

It was abundantly clear that the inhabitants had left in a hurry. There were warm embers in the fireplace and unfinished food on the dishes.

"Let's burn it," Kirre said, after they had secured the surroundings of the house. She didn't dare to do it herself, however, but waited for Aure's decision. Bjorn said nothing; the Kainu knew his opinion.

"Burn it," Aure confirmed.

The Kainu set the largest house on fire and moved off immediately, their purpose being to catch the escaping southerners.

The pursuers soon got proof that they were on the right track. There was a metal buckle on the ground, dropped in a hurry, and further on they found a child's straw doll. The path led the Kainu on toward the south, and they moved rapidly but cautiously, keeping an eye on what was ahead.

The chase continued into the afternoon, with the terrain getting marshier, until finally they reached the edge of the forest. Before their eyes was a wide swamp, with only a few crooked trees growing here and there. Now they knew where the people had escaped to, because in the middle of the swamp was a raised islet that had been surrounded by a simple stockade built to a man's height. The Kainu could see lookouts watching the edge of the forest through the holes in the construction.

The Kainu drew together to decide on how to proceed.

"We must charge from different directions. There can't be many men there. We will surely prevail," said Kirre.

"Many of us will pay with our lives for such folly. We will have to wade through the swamp, across open ground. If they have any skilled archers, their arrows will not miss," replied Vierra, measuring the distance between the forest's edge and the islet.

"We should wait for nightfall. That way, they won't be able to see to shoot. Split up the group and watch from both sides, so they can't escape," Bjorn suggested.

Nobody had a better plan, and they had come so far already. Aure was thoughtful, and looked at the swamp with a mysterious look on her face. She nodded at Bjorn, silently accepting his proposal.

The Kainu dispersed to the forest's edge to form a blockade, so preventing any attempt to escape, and they waited for the night. No one made a run for from the stockade, however, and both sides waited for the dark, in silence.

Finally, the sun set on the horizon, reddening the sky, and the southerners lit a great bonfire in the middle of the stockade. There it glowed, drawing the Kainu like moths to a flame as they waited for darkness and the signal to attack.

Darkness soon took over the swamp. Kirre picked up her drum and started pounding it in an even rhythm. Her example was followed by many others, and the edge of the swamp boomed with the ominous rhythm of drumming, slowly gathering speed. The crescent moon rose to oversee the spectacle that was being played out beneath it. If fear was eating into the southerners' hearts, they didn't try to escape or cry for mercy. Over the noise of the drumming, something that sounded like a night bird's call was suddenly heard, and more than ninety Kainu began simultaneously to cross the swamp to the islet.

They came like the wolves of the forest, crouched and low, and, in the pale light of the moonlit night, they got close to the palisade before they were noticed. Then there was a yell from the walls, and arrows started flying toward the attacking enemy. The Kainu didn't respond by shooting back, but only waded on through the swamp. Only a few were struck by the arrows, more out of bad luck than the accuracy of the archer, before the Kainu arrived on the shore of the islet.

Only then did the Kainu drop their drums and let their own bows sing, directing their shots toward the southern archers who were shooting from behind the poles. Angrily flew the arrows from both sides, with the Kainu barbs mostly striking their intended targets and the southerners missing theirs. The Kainu vastly outnumbered the dozen southern men who were defending the stockade.

Suddenly, the Kainu swarmed over the walls with their knives held between their teeth. As soon as their feet touched the ground, they fell upon the Southern men like wild beasts. For a moment, the defenders held their ground, but soon succumbed to the desperate and blood-filled flurry of the attackers' blades, reflecting the glow of the fire. For years, the Kainu's hatred had grown like a rain-swollen river because of the injustices they had suffered at the hands of the southerners, and now the river of hate burst its banks and flowed over in an uncontrollable torrent of blood.

Vierra was carried along with them, but, while it felt as if her hands were being guided by her brothers' and sisters' hatred, she had the feeling that she was observing all this bloodshed from outside of herself. Had the invaders' slave whips changed her, or was it that she had never really fitted in? The more the southerners' blood was spilled, the less she wanted to be part of it. When it was all over, she just felt a great weariness and an emptiness inside her.

When no opposition remained, and the blood fog lifted from the Kainu's eyes, they looked around. The fire that burned in the middle of the palisade had started to fade, but it still shed enough light to show, huddling as far from the them as possible, a group of frightened women and children. There were about ten women and twenty children, ranging from infants to those of ten summers. Women grasped their children and children their mothers, like a drowning man grabbing the side of a boat. Their eyes looked dazedly at the savages who had just slain their husbands and fathers. Even the smallest children were not crying anymore, even though they had done so during the onslaught. They sensed that their lives were now hanging by threads and, like fawns in high grass, they tried to hide in their mothers' hems and laps, completely still.

But they couldn't hide, and their mothers' hems were no aid against the furious warriors. The majority of the Kainu hesitated, though. The hatred that churned in their minds had started to fade, and they weren't child murderers. However, the toughest and angriest among them hardened their hearts, especially Kirre, who yelled, "What are you waiting for? Finish the job! These children will grow to be new fur-taxers, murderers and plunderers of women. Strike them all to the ground, and the fire will then carry them to the forests of the Underworld, to accompany their dead men!"

No! I will not kill children," Vierra objected. Her will to fight was completely gone, and her thoughts went again along their old, familiar paths. Kirre took a step towards the people who shivered in the middle, her bloody knife held up high.

"You weak fool! I will start the slaughter, if nobody else has the courage."

"They must be killed. The children will grow to be new taxers, new robbers like Kirre said. Even if we don't want to," said Aure. She, too, raised her knife and prepared to finish the job that was still undone.

Then Bjorn stepped toward them and raised his hand as a signal to stop.

"Wait, warriors of Kainu. I have a suggestion. We are not child killers, and there is no point in slaying powerless women, too. You northern sisters and brothers have no use for these people, but we in the south have a lot of burned land to clear, household animals to tend to and crops to thresh, more work than we can do ourselves. Give these children and women to us, and we will raise them to be Kainu, who will never steal women or tax furs. They will grow calluses on their hands from the work, but they'll keep their lives and won't suffer unnecessarily, as long as they work."

"Let them go rather than make them slaves," spat Vierra. Her grim expression revealed her thoughts on this matter. However, she was not in a position to affect the chieftain's decision.

"We will not," said Aure and took a breath. Everyone was ready to hear the chieftain's word.

"Bjorn can keep the women and children. We will take them with us to the north. Here, we will burn everything, the dead southern men and our own fallen sisters and brothers, at sunrise. Everything that's valuable will be evenly divided between those who participated in the battle. Now, let's rest and treat the wounded."

The chieftain's order was the law. The dark night went on, and there was no sign yet of a new day on the skyline.

In the Heart of the Swamp

A cold wind from the east woke Vierra up from her uneasy sleep. Around her, the Kainu slept the restless sleep of those triumphant in the bloodshed. There was only a faint glimmer of light in the eastern sky, like a passing thought that the night might be ending.

Vierra flinched as she heard voices in the dark. Somebody was talking by the fire in hushed tones. Two figures were drawn together against the dim light. Vierra was lying outside of the flickering light of the dying flames. She rolled over and onto her knees, and, taking her spear with her, crawled away into the darkness, making no sound.

The moon provided just enough light for Vierra to see the shadow-like shapes of two people, one large and one small, as they left the camp and walked down from the neck of the land and into the swamp. Vierra followed the figures in the dark like a shadow, wondering how they could see the mires and tussocks in front of them. Vierra could see the black traces of the footprints of the ones she followed, and stepped into them as she walked. She knew that she couldn't cross the swamp on her own in the darkness before dawn.

Her hand found its way to the necklace that was under her fur coat. She had done this many times during the passing days. The touch of the cool bones calmed her nerves. She couldn't understand why someone would go into treacherous ground in the dark like that.

The duo finally stopped in the middle of the swamp. They had walked a good distance away from the dry land and the burned palisade. The shimmer in the eastern sky started to spread, and Vierra could see better around her now. A huge quagmire spread out in front of her eyes. It was like a black, round eye. A hole that led somewhere, a destination which Vierra didn't want to know anything about.

When a voice finally broke the silence, Vierra recognized it as belonging to Aure. Deep inside her she had known who she was following, but for some reason had hoped that it was not so.

"Behold, oh Great Spirit, I have brought a child like we agreed. Will you now give me mine back?"

From somewhere in Aure's direction came the answer, spoken in a shrill, frenzied voice. The inhuman note of the voice echoed in the desolate swamp, so that it was impossible to say exactly where it came from. So repulsive was it, that it raised Vierra's neck hair and filled her mind with uneasiness and fear.

"Only one? I know you have many. I want more, one is not enough."

"But you promised me my youngest daughter back! You said you can bring her back from the Underworld! I have given you so much already – fish, meat, men too." Aure's voice was cracked with pain and despair.

"Dead, already slain men, they've been. Only one was alive and he was ruined with mushroom madness. I want children, lively and fresh. There is power in children that I can use to bring your girl back from the dead. If you bring all the children you have, I will give you all your three daughters."

Aure was silent for a long time and then replied, in a broken voice, "Very well. Here she is, brown-haired and beautiful." And she started to sing, as submissive as only a slave can be.

Spirits of the gloomy swampland
Little people in the deep
Chorus of the helpless children
Victims who the death will keep

Hear me well, my offer take
Down now pull him to you
Eat him with your hungry mouths
All blood, gut and sinew

Give me luck and grant me hope
Give me back what life did steal
Though I come from world above you
All my wounds and ailments heal

The girl, not more than seven summers old, had begun to weep quietly and hopelessly during the song. Aure flicked the hood from her head, revealing her night-black hair that was streaked here and there with white wisps that were clearly visible in the growing eastern light. She knelt on the ground and grabbed the girl around the neck, ready to push her head under the water.

"Let her go!" Vierra's commanding voice concealed the fear that was eating her insides.

Aure twirled around. On her face, the emotions of shame, anger, fear and sorrow succeeded each other in a confusing flurry.

"Go away, please. Let me be in peace. This doesn't concern you." Aure didn't get up, but spread her arms in a pleading gesture. They shook uncontrollably.

"This is madness, I can't just stand and watch," Vierra said.

Aure got up, unsheathing her knife. She stepped toward Vierra in the darkness and the blade flashed as she lifted it, ready to stab. Vierra grabbed her spear with both hands and turned its point towards Aure.

"Knife fights are done for us, cousin. Give up, or do you wish to try your luck against a spear?"

The last sparkle of hope in Aure's eyes died out. For a moment, she just stayed there, immobile. Then suddenly, a high-pitched and unnatural voice yelled, "I do!"

Aure attacked, suddenly and blindly, and surprised Vierra completely. They were separated by the spear that Vierra was steadily holding, however, and it was directed at Aure's stomach. Aure, ignoring the spear, lunged forward with inhuman strength. With a *thunk*, the spear impaled the attacker's stomach but still she came on, the spear-shaft sliding through her body, and attacked Vierra. The battling women reeled and fell into a quagmire, the very same in which Aure had, only minutes earlier, planned to drown the little girl. The girl crawled away from the combatants, but was so stunned that she just watched the fight with huge, frightened eyes.

During the confusion, Aure's knife fell into the water, and she grabbed Vierra by the throat with both hands. Her face was distorted into a grimace of pain and unnatural anger.

Vierra felt like death herself had gone for her throat. The grip was cold and hard as iron, and it froze the blood in the struggling woman's veins. Any thoughts of overpowering Aure escaped her mind and were replaced by blind panic. Try as she might, she could not break the grip around her neck. It would have been easier for a hare to get away from a wolf's jaws. In the quagmire, the water only came halfway up her thigh, but Vierra had the feeling that cold hands were grabbing at her feet, too – hands that dragged her deeper and deeper, into the murky embrace of the swamp. Soon, they were up to their waists in water, then it was up to their necks. And all the time, the inhuman voice sang and screamed.

> *You will see the soul of swampland*
> *Feel the cold inside the earth*
> *Touch of death is on your shoulder*
> *End will bring to warrior's worth*

Vierra couldn't fight anymore, and the water engulfed her completely. For a moment, she felt great relief. How good it would be to take a lungful of swamp water and fall asleep. Leave all this pain behind and meet her late son and husband again. Vierra closed her eyes and got ready to die. The thought of dying didn't make her sad at all. The fighting she-wolf inside her was silent for once, and didn't fight back.

Her hand hit the necklace that was hanging about her neck. Always so cool to the touch, the bones now burned like hot iron. They woke her up from the slumber of horror that she had sunk into.

The spirits flew into the world through the necklace like a river flooding through an ice dam. Vierra saw them only as gray, foggy figures in the black water, but she could feel their ancient strength. Like a tidal wave they went for Aure. The scream that left Aure's lips didn't carry underwater. Vierra, dazed and confused, was overcome with a strange anger.

"Don't help me. I curse you! Why do you help me? I want to go to my loved ones." But not one listened to her pleas.

Vierra suddenly realized she was free. The she-wolf inside her woke up in an instant, and she swam to the surface, convulsing. She gagged and coughed out swamp water as she grabbed for a tussock at the edge of the quagmire.

After taking a few gasps of breath and gathering her strength, Vierra pulled herself out of the mire and looked around. Dawn was lighting up the surroundings, but there were no sounds from the direction of the Kainu camp. She doubted that anyone had seen or heard, from so far away, what had happened in the quagmire. As she lay there amid the silence, it was only the feeble sobbing of the girl that told her that she was still alive.

With a plop, the swamp gave back what it had taken. Vierra's spear protruded from Aure's stomach like a grotesque, crooked mast, and the early morning light made her look bloodied all over. And she was bloody; around her stomach, the water was dark in color, and more blood gushed out of her mouth. Miraculously, she was still alive, coughing up blood and water from inside of her.

Vierra suddenly felt alive again, and she pulled her cousin up. She tried to staunch the bleeding, but the grievous wound was beyond all help. It would pump Aure's life out, one surge after another, until she would finally die.

With a raspy voice, Aure said, "Vierra, I wish you'd let go of my hand all that time ago, so my life wouldn't have ended in shame like this."

"Don't speak, I'll take you back to camp," Vierra said helplessly.

"Flee! The fate of anyone who kills the chieftain is death, and Kirre is the next in line. She will kill someone, even though nobody is guilty. I have disgraced us all." Aure sighed deeply and fell silent. So died the high chieftain of the Kainu, in the arms of her cousin. Vierra and the little girl were left alone.

Finally, Vierra got up and went to the girl, who was coiled upon the ground. She took the girl up into her arms and calmed her, fondling her dirty brown hair. Aure's blood spread from her hands to the hair of the girl, but neither of them cared.

Vierra didn't know if she was comforting the girl, or if it was the other way round. She had imagined that Aure would rule the tribe until her old age. For a moment, she didn't know what to do next.

The sun rose above the horizon and Vierra got up. The words of the First Mother had now come true, and there was no going back to her tribe for her, unless she found a good explanation for what had happened. She decided fast and acted accordingly.

"Girl, can you find your way out of this swamp on your own, to go to your mother?"

"I-I think so."

"Then go. But tell my people that I killed Aure and escaped, and they'll let you back, to be with your own."

"Where will you go then?"

"I don't know. But you haven't seen the last of me yet."

Bjorn's tribe had gone to sleep after a hard day's work. A light summer wind blew silently, and the birds that had returned to the land of the Kainu chirped in chorus at the joy of a new, sunny season. The summer's hut-camp had been built near the swidden, away from their log houses which they would once more return to in the winter, in the annual struggle against the cold.

The slaves slept in a large, roughly made lean-to. The women were tied up as a precaution, in case they were entertaining hopes of escape and freedom. The children were free and slept close to the sides of their mothers, looking for at least a moment's comfort from the cold world. The Kainu didn't bother to guard the slaves, as their dogs would foil any attempt at escape.

Yet, in the dead of night, a figure, silent as a shadow, emerged from the forest. It was as if the forest had conjured it out of its depths, for it moved so quietly that even the dogs didn't wake to bark at the intruder. One by one, she went to every sleeping dog, and left behind a carcass. So skillfully did she carry out her work of death that neither the camp's inhabitants, nor those dogs that were still alive, woke to it. When even those dogs lay dead, the figure sneaked into the slaves' lean-to. Once again, a knife flashed in the night, and the leather leashes that held the women were severed. They didn't need any words, and in complete silence the group sneaked out of the camp and into the dark forest, carrying their children with them.

The shadowy figure led the group on through the forest, to where she had stashed food for their journey home.

"This will be enough to get you south, back to your homeland."

"Aren't you coming with us?" one of the women asked.

"No, I still have to go back north." The stranger touched a necklace on her neck, which was made of countless different bones.

"Who are you, and why do you help us?"

The stranger stroked her black hair, which was tied back, smiled sternly and replied:

"I am someone who knows the curse of slavery. Keep going and do not stop, for the night is waning."

Pathfinders

The Red-haired Prisoner

HE EARLY autumn's sweltering day was the summer's last breath against the cold face of the approaching winter. The leaves, already bitten by a few freezing nights, had started to change their color, and there was a damp whiff of the cool night dew lingering in the air. An exceptionally warm southern wind smiled together with the sun, making the travelers who walked between the great pines sweat.

The rugged men didn't fit in with the surrounding scenery. Their clothes, gait and movement told of clumsiness and foreignness. One could see from their faces that they felt the same hatred and rejection toward the forest that it seemed to emanate toward them.

The first one was a large, fat man. His bald head shone with sweat, and the strain of walking made him pant. His limbs were like tree trunks and it was apparently arduous to move them. His thin beard proved that hair, long gone from his crown, didn't grow much better under his chin, either. The forest of large, mature trees was easy to traverse, but still he stumbled over roots and branches now and then. None of the others made fun of his clumsiness, though.

If any of the men was at home in the forest, it was the young man who walked behind the leader. He was a head taller than the man in front of him, although he was also slighter in all possible ways. His sand-colored hair had been combed back and his beard, even lighter in color, was groomed and cut.

"Starkhand, when will we reach the shore?" he asked the bald man ahead of him.

"Tomorrow morning. We'd be there already if they hadn't broken the boat," the fat man snorted and pointed to the brothers that walked behind them. They denied the act as if with one voice.

They could have been twins as they were almost indistinguishable. Both had slouched shoulders and sand-brown hair that was an untidy mess of curls. They wore leather clothes that had seen better days and spoke to each other quietly, without pause.

Between them walked a bound woman, who was as different from them as a fox from a pack of rabid dogs. Her rich red hair was knotted and smeared with soot and her pretty, round face was covered in streaks of dirt and tears. There was a grubby piece of cloth rammed in her mouth and held in place by a leather strap that was tied tightly around her head. Her leather clothes, which were decorated with elaborate patterns and hung with pieces of bone and small stones, had suffered tears and rips from her having been manhandled and dragged through the forest.

"Shall we eat for a change?" yelled one of the brothers to the duo that walked before them.

The large man stopped and turned.

"We won't get to the shore by eating," he snorted, but sat on the ground anyway and leaned back against a sturdy pine. "Take the rag off its mouth and give it food. They don't pay us for dead ones in the slave market."

The large man directed his words toward the young man, who walked cautiously over to the red-haired woman.

"Try to bewitch me, and I'll cut off your tongue," the young man hissed. He removed the leather strap and the woman immediately spat the rag out of her mouth. She flexed her jaws, which had been numbed by the grip of the gag.

Pitiful scraps of dried food were eaten in silence, except for the brothers who continued with their meaningless babble. A raven croaked somewhere high above, in the tall pines.

The group continued their journey. When the afternoon began to turn into evening, the pine forest started to give way to other trees. At first, the pine trees just grew smaller, but soon thin birches and other deciduous trees pushed themselves among them. Ahead of them, the terrain grew steeper and formed a hill, the slopes of which were completely covered in birches. The croaking of the raven was continuous now, and made the men stare into the trees, searching for the bird.

"Show yourself, and I'll stop your screeching," the young man stated, fiddling with his bow. He was the only member of the group to carry one.

They heard the swish too late. An arrow with goose-feather fletching struck the young man's thigh, sticking out of it like a crooked feather. The man cried out, gasped and convulsively grabbed the arrow that had appeared in his leg. The others threw themselves to the ground, looking wildly in the direction the arrow had come from.

Their eyes met only the calm forest of the afternoon. Not even a rustle of a twig betrayed the location of the shooter. Starkhand yelled from the ground to the brothers:

"Find the fiend and kill it!"

The brothers looked at each other without moving. Starkhand pulled a rusty shortsword from his belt.

"Now!"

The men got up reluctantly and looked around, scared. As no more arrows came their way, they started to walk cautiously toward the forest, in the direction from which the arrow had come.

"Show me that arrow," Starkhand growled, getting up with difficulty. He walked over to the young man, who held his leg in agony. The large man felt around the wound for a moment with rough, experienced hands.

"A notched head. I can't get it out without cutting it. When we reach the shore, I can dig it out, but after that you won't be able to walk for a long time. Now, I'll just cut the shaft and you'll have to try…"

The sentence was interrupted by a muffled cry of pain from the forest. It was followed by a scream of rage that ended in a croak. In a split second, the silent forest had become filled with brooding shadows. Amid the trees, a silent and merciless death waited for them.

Starkhand and the wounded man looked at each other for a moment. Starkhand grabbed the red-haired woman by the arm and dragged her to her feet. He half carried and half dragged the woman along with him as they started to flee through the woods without looking back.

Despite his burden, Starkhand soon outdistanced the injured man. The slower man wept and gnashed his teeth as he tried to keep up with Starkhand, but it was futile. Soon, the large man heard the familiar scream of death behind him.

Sweat burst off Starkhand's brow and hands in streams, and he stopped running. Shaking, he turned around and waited with the red-haired prisoner under his arm, for what was to follow. He didn't have to wait for long.

A black-haired woman stepped out of the woods. A few beads of sweat sparkled on her forehead, but no other signs of fatigue were visible. Breathing evenly, she sang, in a clear, effortless voice.

Death by my hand for you, stranger
Wretched scoundrel goes to ground
Writhe there with the hungry earthworms
Until no more flesh is found

The words were carried along with a hunting bow that was ready to fire, the arrowhead pointed straight and unwaveringly toward the large man's chest. The woman watched Starkhand along the shaft of the arrow.

It wasn't the first time Starkhand had met death eye to eye. Licking his lips, he pushed his red-haired prisoner aside.

"Let's settle this with these." He tapped the shortsword on his belt. "It seems like you have a blade of your own on your belt."

She responded with laughter. Starkhand rushed forward, drawing his weapon. He never even got within fighting range.

Old Friends

A campfire that burned in the evening gloom flared warmth to the faces of the silent women who sat by it.

The usually talkative Rika was silent, following the enthusiastic gratitude she bestowed on the black-haired woman for saving her life. Her hands shook as she put pieces of the fish, caught and cooked by Vierra, into her mouth.

"Who were those men?" Rika finally asked, in a trembling voice.

"Slavers. They follow the rivers inland, looking for people to grab and sell as slaves either beyond the sea or to Turian witches," said Vierra, glancing up from whittling a piece of wood. "What on earth are you doing here, so far from home?"

Rika's dark stare and squeezed fists told Vierra that she shouldn't ask any more questions. They were silent for a moment.

"Vierra..." Rika's voice held a wary tone, which was rare for her. "Is it true what they say? The ones that came back from the war?"

"Well, what did they tell you?"

"That you killed Aure."

Vierra threw some pieces of wood she had whittled into the fire and was silent for a moment. Finally, she nodded. Rika's anguished expression told her that this was not what she had wanted to hear.

"Why?"

"I had no choice. It wasn't Aure that I killed. It was something else, something dark."

"What do you mean? An evil spirit? Why didn't I notice anything different about her?"

"How should I know?" Vierra answered, with an involuntary snap. "Maybe you had something else on your mind."

Rika's angst flamed quickly to anger. "So you mean that I don't have what it takes to be a witch, is that it?"

"Even witches make mistakes."

"You've been named as a traitor of the tribe. I should try to kill you with my bare hands for what you did."

Vierra smiled a stern, cold smile. "The men who captured you tried, they each had a turn."

Rika shuddered, and she huffed audibly. "Could you try to explain?"

Vierra shook her head. "I couldn't, even if I wanted to, and I don't want to go back there even in my mind."

"But then you can't return to the tribe anymore."

"True, I can't."

"Then why did you come?"

"Because of this," Vierra said and lifted up the necklace that she'd been carrying under her moose skin jacket. It was skillfully constructed from countless claws and teeth of different animals, and wearing it made Vierra look like a chieftain. She took the necklace slowly from her neck, briefly remembering something that had happened a long time ago. "I know how important this is to you."

Vierra presented the necklace to Rika. In the campfire, the resinous wood crackled and sent clouds of sparks up into the dark evening every now and then. Rika reluctantly took the necklace from Vierra's hands. "Thank you."

She placed the necklace around her neck as she gazed silently at the fire.

"Where will you go?"

"I will take you back to our tribe's lands. After that, who knows?" Vierra looked at the treetops, which were barely visible in the dark. "Let's go to sleep now. Tomorrow will be a long day."

Without saying any more, she wrapped herself in her furs and lay down beside the fire. Rika remained sitting by the campfire, eating the remainder of her fish. She had always been a slow eater when it came to fish, as she was afraid she'd get bones stuck in her throat.

For a moment, she looked at her friend who was already twitching in her sleep.

Rika was about to say something, but then just sighed and lay down on her side of the fire. She turned around many times before falling asleep.

The morning sun glimmered in the trees and slowly dried the rich dew that the autumn night had given. Vierra and Rika were doing their chores, huffing with the cold of the night. They rubbed their hands, stiff and cold because of the damp, together over the embers of last night's campfire, and got ready to leave.

Vierra tried the traps she had left around their camp. One small hare had strayed into one of the traps, providing a little food for the speedy return home. Rika watched from the side as Vierra handled the animal with confident hands.

"Always a hunter," Rika muttered silently to herself. Not silently enough, though.

"You're still punishing yourself over that?" Vierra asked.

"How could I forget?" And Rika sang:

> *Forest is the place for Kainu*
> *Blessed be the use of bow*
> *Flesh of game, the sweetest trophy*
> *Fishes fatter make us grow*

"How about this one?" Vierra replied with her own song.

> *Best of luck is witches' council*
> *Theirs to know is birth and name*
> *May their souls wax old and mellow*
> *Source of our tribe's flame*

"Yes," Rika admitted with a sigh. She fiddled with the necklace that hung from her neck, without noticing she was doing it. "Shall we?"

They traveled as fast as Rika, much the slower of the two, could manage. They were traveling back down the same path that the men had used the day before, with Rika as their prisoner.

The warm, sunny autumn weather made their trip pleasant, and late in the afternoon they stopped by a small creek, to eat the hare they had caught that morning. They roasted the meat on sticks in a fire while gazing at the pleasant creek view. The trees on the riverbank had already dropped the first of their leaves, which floated on the surface of the water, slowly moving toward the sea that waited downstream.

"Tomorrow, we'll reach Kainu lands," Rika said, while gnawing on a piece of meat on the stick.

Vierra looked at the river. "Could you go alone from here to our people?"

"At least come a bit further with me." Rika's gaze followed some leaves that swam away from them. "Where will you go?"

There was a long silence. Then Vierra replied, "I don't know, but I've known for a long time that I would have to leave some day."

Rika wiped her eyes surreptitiously, so that her companion, lost in her thoughts, would not notice.

"Shall we continue?" Rika asked and got up unnecessarily fast.

Their route now left the path that Rika and the men had followed before. The orienteer in Vierra said that by doing that, they would reach their tribe faster.

The pathless wilderness took them toward a large ridge, the slopes of which were completely covered by a dark spruce forest. They approached it diagonally and soon started to go up the brae, overhung with those evergreen trees.

After reaching the summit, they took a moment to catch their breath. Up there, the forest was sparse and the earth rocky. Wherever they turned their eyes they could see wilderness, marked by ridges, valleys and lakes and bordered in one direction by the billowing sea.

Vierra took a deep breath, as if trying to draw it all inside her, to store everything she could see, hear, smell or feel in her heart. The thought of leaving it all pressed heavily on her shoulders. Rika walked beside her and wrapped her arms around her friend. They stood there for a long time without saying a word, just staring into the distance.

"Remember how we used to climb dunes and hills?" Rika finally said, breaking the silence. Vierra smiled for a moment and, for the first time in a long while, that smile held not a trace of bitterness.

"Those were good times," Rika agreed, without waiting for Vierra's answer. "Nobody mocked me then."

"You weren't mocked. At least, not after a few of them had been given black eyes!" Vierra said.

"Maybe not out loud, but I knew what they all thought. Red-haired orphan stranger who can't hunt and who the old witch took in only because she felt sorry for her."

Vierra didn't answer. She was a bad liar.

"Have I ever asked why you didn't join in with the other bullies?"

"We were both strangers, in our own way. But when Eera leaves, you'll be a witch and you won't be a stranger anymore. I shall be happy about that. Let's continue."

Vierra started to walk down from the top of the rocky ridge. Behind her, Rika sighed deeply, but the wind, roaming around the hilltop, consumed the sound.

Under the slope, an oval lake surrounded by a fair grove opened out before the travelers. The sun, moving toward evening, threw its last rays upon the lake's surface, and the travelers descended rapidly along the slope and toward the shore. The forest was so thick along the shore that they had to work really hard in order to reach the water. Here and there, large mushrooms grew in the forest like red-white bobbles.

"Snake mushrooms," Rika stated and tried her best to avoid the branches which Vierra, who walked ahead of her, bent and released toward her without meaning to.

"Didn't you eat them at one time? I had never seen Eera so angry before."

"I did, but I don't want to remember that."

"Snake mushroom, the mushroom of the witch. You must have eaten them many times since then."

"Well, of course I have."

Vierra disappeared into an especially strong thicket. From there, however, she hissed a warning to the woman following her. Rika crouched down into the bushes and tried to see what had caused this change in her companion's behavior.

Before them, the beach opened up. The surrounding thicket had been chopped down and long, straight wooden poles were lying on the ground. They had apparently been used as support beams for a lean-to. Neither the hut skins nor the dwellers were anywhere to be seen, but here and there on the ground were eating utensils and other goods, left behind for some reason when the camp was abandoned.

The reason for Vierra's warning became obvious when Rika saw a large number of ducks walking around in the glade and swimming in the lake, near the shore. Vierra had already armed her bow and approached them slowly, sneaking from one shadow to another and looking for a position to shoot from.

The bow sang, and the arrow it had sent impaled an unsuspecting bird. The others rose to their wings in the blink of an eye, and the calm beach turned into a flapping chaos of birds. Vierra's bow spoke again, and a bird that had already taken off spiraled slowly down to the ground, one wing pierced by an arrow. Vierra dashed after it and soon returned, both ducks dangling from her hand.

"Tonight we feast on fowl," she stated.

"This isn't a Kainu camp," Rika replied, changing the subject abruptly.

"Maybe Turian, they've left in a hurry. Look, there's an intact clay pot, we can boil the meat."

"And there's a pile of rocks, where we can make a fire for cooking and to warm the night."

"And in the morning I will go. You can make it to our tribe's lands from here by yourself."

"Wouldn't you come just a bit further with me?"

Vierra looked at the sky: in the western horizon, above the setting sun, a large front of clouds was forming. Like a grim salute from winter, it engulfed the sun and they felt the air turn colder.

"Can you make the fire? There seems to be firewood there. I'll go and collect twigs, because it looks like we'll need shelter very soon."

They did their chores promptly, glancing at the approaching clouds now and then. The evening had darkened toward night by the time they had built a makeshift shelter out of the twigs and wood that lay around the clearing. They built it as close to the crude fireplace as possible, where a joyful fire already flared in the center of the big rocks. Vierra cleaned the birds and plucked most of the feathers before placing the prey in the pot of boiling water, adding plants and herbs that they'd gathered from the forest to flavor the stew.

The birds were soon cooked, and the women ate with a good appetite. In the meantime, the curtain of clouds had covered the whole sky and when the sun had set, darkness descended over their campfire. It didn't rain, though, only a few drips here and there, and the women were able to carry out their chores by the fire in peace.

"I brought you something from the forest that you can take to Eera as a gift, when you go back to the tribe."

Vierra took out a number of white-stemmed mushrooms, the red caps of which were dotted with white flecks, which she apparently picked in between her chores.

"Take them away!" Rika yelled angrily.

Vierra looked at her, astonished. "What's wrong? The snake mushroom is the mushroom of the witch."

Like a stream in springtime which breaks the ice, Rika finally started her lament.

"I'm not a witch, and I can't take mushrooms to Eera, because Eera is dead. She died after midsummer, during the heat. She died and couldn't even begin her last journey. And I haven't been chosen. The spirits haven't accepted me and I've made no journeys. Not after I fooled around as a child and wanted to talk to the spirits, like Eera."

Rika shuddered and twisted her hands, as tears flowed down her cheeks. Vierra didn't dare interrupt the flood of words.

"Everything would have been fine if I hadn't given you the necklace. Without it, I couldn't do the witches' journey and Eera was angry that she could not go on her final one. She relented in time and we waited for you to return from war, with the necklace. But Kaira came alone and didn't want to say anything about what had happened. The only thing we got out of him was that Aure had died and you were to blame. I started on a new necklace, but you need so many bones to make one."

Rika took a deep, gasping breath in order to continue.

"Eera got sick, and the plant spirits wouldn't help. She wanted me to do the witches' journey without a necklace, but I didn't dare." Rika was racked with unrestrained weeping and for a moment she couldn't speak.

"We argued and I ran away. I wish I'd listened to her. The next time I saw her, she was on her deathbed and we had no witch to hasten her journey."

Vierra didn't answer. Over the wind and the crackling of the fire, only Rika's now subdued sobbing could be heard.

"I'm no comforter, you know that," said Vierra. "I couldn't return even if I wanted to. How on earth did you end up as the prisoner of those men? I returned alone to give you the necklace, and ran into a member of our tribe. From her, I heard that you had wandered away, and I came after you."

"I left. I thought it was all the same if I died in the forest. A red-haired apprentice of a witch, who's not a witch and can't hunt. There's no use for me. Then I stumbled upon those four men by the riverside, who were sitting by a fire near their boat. They drank beer and had food and..." Rika swallowed for a moment before continuing. "They promised to take me with them. But then they tied me up and told me I was to be sold as a slave to the Vikings."

A red flush of shame rose to Rika's face; to be fooled like that was almost as bad as being captured.

Vierra nodded.

"Did you destroy their boat?" Rika asked.

"Yes. I believe that living as a Vikings' slave would not suit you." Vierra's cold smile had returned to her face. "Now you have a necklace. Can't you do the journey?"

"But I have no helper, no protector for my body if I go. And I'm afraid. I haven't traveled since that one time, and Eera can't help me any more if something goes wrong."

"Do you know how to do it?"

"Well, I do, but what does it help if..."

"If it's all the same if you die, why are you afraid? What does it matter if you die on your journey or in the hands of slavers? And I can protect your body if you tell me what to do."

Rika wiped her eyes. "Are you serious?"

Vierra took one of the snake mushrooms and cut a piece off it, offering it to Rika. "Start chewing, then."

Rika's face cracked into an involuntary smile.

"You can't do it like that. Put water in the pot and add the mushrooms. You have to boil them first, because the spirit of the snake is strong and it will make the eater very sick. The one to go on the journey must know the song for the birth of the snake. Otherwise you can't control the journey, and the journey will control you. And a drum is needed as well. Give me those two branches."

"What does the protector have to do?"

"When I travel, no other living being must see me. You need to keep them away from me, otherwise they will take my empty shell for themselves. And if I get lost, Eera would have come after me and guided me back."

"That I can't do, so it's best that you get back by yourself."

"Oh, and when I travel, whatever you do, don't look into my eyes."

"Why not?"

"If you do so, you will be in control of my body and I won't be able to return. And your spirit is not ready to rule over two bodies. Do as I say."

The tears and smile on Rika's face conflicted with each other. And the anxiousness in her eyes would have been obvious to anyone.

The Journey

It seemed to Vierra that Rika had been drumming forever. Rika had eaten the mushrooms once they had completed their lengthy boiling, but nothing seemed to be happening yet. Rika had sat there the whole time, looking into the fire while she drummed the branches against each other in an even, hypnotic rhythm. The sky seemed to be waiting and kept its rain to itself, while the thick clouds kept the stars and the moon from seeing what was going on beneath them.

Rika had covered her face with mud that she'd dug from the beach sand. On her bare upper body she had painted spirals, birds, ships and wind with charcoal, to speed the journey. Her beautiful red hair glowed in the campfire, as if it, too, was on fire.

Vierra shook her head. She felt as if the drumming was starting to sink into her consciousness, as she was no longer sure which direction the sound was coming from. It strengthened and diminished in turns, even though Rika's hands struck the branches together with even strength. Vierra looked at her friend's face, but her eyes were fixed on the fire. There was a strange glow in them. Suddenly, Rika started to sing.

> *Serpent-kin now hear my song*
> *Feel the power in these words*
> *I know how you came to being*
> *I can cut life off your cords*
>
> *Bird of old, of stone and sea*
> *Again he built his nest*
> *In which golden eggs he planted*
> *On top of hay's soft rest*

Just one egg held all the wisdom
Knowledge imbued the other
Steadiness of hand and mind
Bristled from their brother

Hatching them, the bird was thirsty
Hunger lived inside of him
So he flew off to the seaside
To catch some fish on ocean grim

Creepy snake who hid in shadows
To the nest he scoured
Took the eggs of grace and virtue
All of them devoured

Bird came from the restless ocean
He saw what the snake had done
His might rose from calmed waters
Angry song in there begun

Stronger grew the mighty song
The song of hate and scorn
It could cut like sharpest blade
Soon legs of snake were shorn

One and two and three and four
Cut the song of might
Until the snake had legs no more
Grounded him outright

To the worm he plainly said
"I'll scorn you forever
Broke my nest and ate my eggs
Again shall walk you never"

From his belly, snake just said
"Keep my legs, I care not
I have all your knowledge now
All your skills I have caught"

So the snake did slide away
On his belly crawled
Never saw his legs again
Went his way appalled

Vierra recognized the song of snake's birth, and she got to hear countless other animals have their turn after that. Beads of sweat started to gather on Rika's face, but neither the strength of the song nor the rhythm of the drum faded. She was showing the measure of her skill and knowledge as the night drew on, and still the branches kept striking each other in an even rhythm.

Suddenly, the drumming stopped. Vierra started and noticed that Rika had fallen onto her back. She writhed for a moment and then just lay there, her eyes looking into eternity, unblinking.

Vierra pushed her ear to the chest of the collapsed woman and heard her heartbeat. She also heard her faint breathing, so she knew Rika was still alive. Vierra half carried, half dragged her unconscious friend to the lean-to, farther from the fire, and sat beside the empty body. She did all this while making sure that she kept her gaze away from the red-haired woman's eyes.

Every breath seemed so long, and every passing moment seemed to stretch with them. Vierra kept listening to the sound of Rika's breathing and the sound of her heart beating while she waited for her to return from her journey. As time passed, her concern grew, as Rika showed no signs of regaining consciousness. The eastern horizon had started to brighten when Vierra finally made her decision. And, as always, she executed it fast.

Rika hadn't eaten all of the mushrooms they'd boiled. The rest remained in the now cooled pot beside the campfire. Vierra dug the mushrooms from the pot and ate them as fast as possible. The taste was horrible, but it didn't stop her. She grabbed the branches Rika had dropped and started to drum them, trying to imitate her friend's rhythm.

Soon, she realized that even though the boiling had weakened the snake's spirit, the mushrooms were still too strong for her, for she had no experience of witches' work. Her stomach roiled with disgust, and she had to use all her willpower not to vomit the mushrooms out. Grinding her teeth and beating the branches against each other, she managed to keep the spirits inside her.

Vierra felt tremendously thirsty, but she didn't dare stop drumming or take her eyes away from the fire. Suddenly, the air seemed thick, and Vierra had to gasp for each breath. Streams of sweat flowed down her face and hands, but she didn't notice.

All at once, the sky started to throw water down at Vierra. The rainfall rang loudly in her ears and the crashing sound of falling water cut through her until she was sure her head would crack. There was no way to escape, however, and she kept looking at the fire and drumming. Soon, she was soaking wet and water dripped continuously from her black hair. The flame Vierra looked at started to stretch and jump, and it was hard to keep her eyes focused on it.

The whispers were muffled at first, so quiet that Vierra wasn't sure if she'd imagined them. Soon, the sounds grew louder and the shadow of her doubt dissipated. She strained to hear but couldn't make out what the speakers were saying. There were dozens of voices and they all spoke at once.

"Be silent or speak in turns," Vierra finally snapped impatiently.

For a moment the voices paused, and then they answered with a clear voice.

"You summoned us yourself, from a place where there is no return. Why can't you bear the consequences of your actions?" It was Aure's voice. Vierra could almost see her stubborn cousin saying those words.

"Speak one at a time, so I can answer." Vierra wiped sweat off her forehead.

"All right. Me first," Aure continued. "I have nothing to say. You did what you had to do, and I hold no grudge against you."

The voices spoke, each in their turn. Some were calm and serious like Aure, others angry and bitter because of the fate they had suffered. They asked Vierra why she had killed them, and she answered all of them. None of the voices were able to say what she could have done differently. The questioning lasted a long time, because Vierra had sent many spirits into the Underworld over the years.

"Why didn't you stay with us and celebrate?" a small voice asked finally. It took Vierra's breath away, and the tears that had been absent for so long rose to her eyes. During the long, dark years that had passed, she had forgotten what her son's voice sounded like. Now, after all this time, it cut her soul like a searing blade. Vierra couldn't answer.

"Yes, why not? You might have been able to help us escape," said Vaaja, her dead husband, in his turn.

"How could I have known?" Vierra slurred painfully. "I wouldn't have left if I had known. Just say it, ask it of me and I'll come to you. My blade will cut my own flesh like it cuts my enemies."

Vierra crawled along the shore, shaking, until she found her blade. She held it against her throat. Her hands shook uncontrollably in the storm of emotions which had been held at bay for so long.

"Hold!" The yell that cut the air accepted no argument. "Put the knife down before you commit any more foolish acts."

Vierra dropped her knife as she saw who had stepped into the campfire's circle of light. The First Mother hadn't changed. The same wrinkly, naked body, the same piercing gaze. The same voice, which demanded that you listen and obey without hesitation.

Vierra's frustrations burst out. How many hardships had she faced? She cursed the Mother, and the destiny she had set for her so long ago. "You and your destiny!" she yelled, right in the old woman's face. "Why will you not let me die, or else allow me to be happy?"

"Happiness is a privilege of the few and of the mad," the elder answered. "Do you really think that I'm behind all the adversity you have faced and still have to face?"

"You and you alone. Everything has gone wrong since I met you. My son died, my husband died, the Vikings took me. Where's the greatness that you foretold for me?"

"Somewhere there, hidden by your own stupidity," the First Mother said, taking in the night-darkened land with a sweep of her gnarled hand. "Who told you to take a man who was persecuted by a Turian witch? Who told you to attack the Vikings with no consideration for yourself? You could have shot them from the cover of the forest and kept your freedom, but you didn't want to."

Vierra swallowed, looking for an excuse. "I had nothing left."

"You had yourself. Yourself, but you don't value that. If you don't get what you want, you won't take anything. None of us gets what we want, ever, and even the greatest of us have to get used to that. You've always wanted to protect children. How many could you have saved while you languished in the Vikings' houses, sweeping floors and warming the beds of your masters?"

"Then what should I do? Be selfish?"

"I will reveal a secret to you, since you don't seem to understand it by yourself. Everyone else puts themselves first. If you don't do it, too, you will walk the world from one misery to another, and your old sufferings will be just a pale reminder of what the vast world can give to the Fargoer."

"Then what –"

The old woman interrupted Vierra by slapping her on the face with an open palm. The Mother's other hand grabbed Vierra's throat with an iron grip.

"You will take the world by the throat and force it to give you what you want. You'll cut your way through with blade and bow and the skills you have been given. And whenever possible, help others the best you can. But you will not sacrifice yourself, not for those who do not see your value. Now, get out of my face, you Bringer of Disappointment." The Mother pushed Vierra away, and she fell on her back at the edge of the campfire's circle of light.

Vierra tried to answer the Mother, but the whole world around her started to fade and bend. It plunged erratically, and she shook her head to try and clear it. Her struggling was in vain, however. Vierra felt as if she was falling through the woods and sinking into the ground on which her body was lying.

She suddenly found herself looking down at her own body from high in the air. It lay unmoving in the flickering light of the campfire, green eyes open but unseeing. Indeed she was not a witch, and her spirit, disconnected from her body, was like a leaf in autumn that had been ripped away from a tree, for the wind to take where it wanted to. She was yanked away, and from the heights she saw the rising sun in the east, shedding its first rays through the tattered clouds.

One delirious image after another flashed before her eyes. They came with a stunning clarity, merging into each other, and afterward she could only remember a small part of them. Beneath her, she saw a tapestry of dunes and lakes. It was the land she used to call home, but it was soon far away in the distance as her spirit flew from it, faster than any bird could fly.

She arrived at the shore of a great sea, where long Viking ships split the water. Even further she went, beyond the forests behind the sea and cities filled with people. She cringed at their crowds and strangeness.

Her spirit kept going on, toward the south, showing her cities with dreamy palaces with water flowing through them beneath the glowing sun. Beyond a blue sea, she saw an expanse of yellow sand littered with strange, hunchbacked creatures, which walked its paths guided by sand-colored people.

Even farther her spirit flew, into deep-green, impenetrable forests that were filled with intoxicating voices. Ruins made of green stone stood in the center of the forest, and someone sang a spell in a language that was already old when the first men were born.

Her spirit rose higher and higher, until she could see the world curving underneath her and, outside it, the black, endless sea of the beginning. There the world floated, one of the shards of the broken egg of the seagull, among others. Nothing lit that black sea and Vierra felt rather than saw the huge entity that engulfed her on all sides.

Her longing for distant lands and her desire for adventure were extinguished by fear and loneliness. There was no way that she could return to her own world. She had no strength to turn the wind that blew her spirit forth.

Then she saw a bird coming from far away. It was a huge eagle-owl, its feathers glowing red from the sun shining behind it. The bird snatched her up in its claws as easily as it would have taken a mouse, and started to fly back down, towards home, with strong wings. Wind whistled in Vierra's ears, but she felt warm and calm.

"I should have known that you didn't have the patience to just sit beside me," the great owl stated. Its voice was Rika's voice.

"I couldn't just idly watch. I wanted to help."

The owl laughed. Vierra wondered how an owl could do that. The wings carried her back towards home. They flew through the land which was bathed in the morning sun, all the way to the lonely beach, where Vierra once again saw herself lying on the ground.

The owl landed beside Rika's and Vierra's unconscious bodies.

"It's time to go back," the bird said. "Time to move on."

Vierra looked at herself, lying there, and looked into her own eyes. She fell with increasing speed toward their green depths. The eyes filled her consciousness and for a moment, she felt a ripping apart of the worlds of body and spirit. Her yell of panic faded into darkness.

Vierra woke up with a sigh. Her eyes hurt and her head felt dizzy. Her cheek was sore where the Mother's hand had struck her. She opened her eyes and Rika was there, huffing because of the cold, her red hair in disarray. But Rika gave her a broad smile, and she seemed to brim with her old confidence once more.

"Come and warm yourself by the fire," Rika said, guiding Vierra, who was still groggy.

Morning sun lit the half-cloudy sky and cool land. Summer's struggles were over, and the wind that now blew carried with it a taste of autumn and coming change.

"Did it work?" Vierra managed to ask, once the worst of the numbness and cold had started to leave her limbs and mind.

"It did. Thank you, friend. Without you, it wouldn't have been possible."

Both were silent for a long time. They knew that the steps they had taken during the night would now take them away from each other. The morning passed, and they just fed the fire and tried to make the moment last as long as possible.

Finally, Vierra got up and turned to look at Rika.

"Now you can go back home. I must leave."

"I know. Yesterday, I wouldn't have understood, but now I do. I will give you a piece of advice, even though I probably shouldn't, and even though I don't understand everything that was shown to me during my journey."

Rika was silent for a moment, searching her mind for the right words. Apparently she couldn't find them, because finally, she just said: "Don't die."

"What does that mean?" Vierra asked.

"I mean, don't die far from home. If you do that, you'll never see the fires of the Underworld and meet your son and husband."

Normally, Vierra might have been angered by such talk. However now, after the journey, her mind was strangely light. The path ahead of her looked clearer and brighter, and the burden of the past felt less heavy.

"We'll see each other again," Vierra said, with a hint of a question in her voice.

"Yes," Rika answered. "We will see one another again before the end."

Vierra looked at her friend and then turned her eyes toward the south. She sang brightly toward the rising day:

I can feel the air of south-lands
Breeze so lovely on my face
Restless are my legs beneath me
Bid to vanish with no trace

Winds of wonder carry whispers
Sounds of spirits wild and free
I will hear their call to wander
See what fate they hold for me

This time, she was ready to go.

The Birth of Kainu

Before a time, before a place
Before the man and beast
The endless sea, so dark and vast
Reached round from west to east

From the depths now grew a cliff
A cliff so big and white
Rising from the shoreless sea
A shard in ocean's might

All alone were sea and stone
Until the Seagull came
A bird of sea, a bird of stone
Without a home or name

He found the stone, he found the cliff
He laid his nest in peace
At last, he thought, the time has come
The endless search will cease

But bitter was the lonely sea
Its hate flowed cold and dark
It raised a wave from murky depths
Destruction at its mark

There was the rock, there was the nest
All torn down with the wave
It blew the nest and blew the bird
Took eggs to watery grave

The bird of sea, the bird of stone
Rose high on wings of gold
He opened up his beak and let
His magic song unfold

His golden eggs all torn and wet
Transformed beneath his might
To earth and sky he changed them all
To shine he made sun bright

All of this and so much more
He built with words said true
The land of life, the land of death
All this his magic grew

There was the world, so beautiful
So beautiful but bare
He took the final golden egg
Caressed it with much care

From it, he drew the best of all
His work of finest birth
A beast, a bird, a fish in sea
All beings on this earth

Then he did it all again
For we all need a mate
But when he got to humankind
Wise bird could see our fate

"You shall walk this earth alone
I shall not give a bride
You'll bring forth the great turmoil
That lasts till all have died"

So it was the bitter man
Went on his way alone
Fishing in the empty sea
With endless wail and groan

"Oh, I am the poorest soul
Without a love or care
Fishes rotting in the sun
And no one here to share"

Suddenly from darkest sea
An eerie voice did say
"I can make a woman too
But there's a price to pay

She will be fine, she will be fair
She is what you have craved
She has a mind of sharpened blade
She has your soul enslaved

She cooks your fish, she makes you strong
She burns your love as fuel
You shall do everything she wants
Your people, she will rule

Shall I give this woman then
Creature of highest might
To carry and give birth to you
To be your brightest light?"

Man was eager to respond
"I want her as my own
Unite us now, O eerie voice
I loathe to live alone"